The Dictionary of Urdu Poetry

For Shaayari Lovers

2500+ Must-know Urdu Words from 6000 Top Shers by 50 Master Shaayars

From Mir and Ghalib to Faraz and Shakir

Urdu words in Engish and Hindi script :

Meanings in English

The Dictionary of Urdu Poetry

For Shaayari Lovers

2500+ Must-know Urdu Words from 6000 Top Shers by 50 Master Shaayars

From Mir and Ghalib to Faraz and Shakir

Urdu words in Engish and Hindi script : Meanings in English

Sunil Gupta 'Mustaqil'

ZORBA BOOKS

Published by Zorba Books, June 2022
Website: www.zorbabooks.com
Email: info@zorbabooks.com
Author Name : Sunil Gupta

Title:- **The Dictionary of Urdu poetry**
Printbook ISBN :- 978-93-93029-13-3
Ebook ISBN :- 978-93-93029-15-7

Zorba Books Pvt. Ltd. (opc)
Sushant Arcade,
Next to Courtyard Marriot,
Sushant Lok 1, Gurgaon – 122009, India

DEDICATED TO

Shalini

MY WIFE AND CHEERLEADER

Ham-safar chahiye hujum nahin
Ek musafir bhi qafila hai mujhe
Ahmad Faraz

Aadmi kya vo na samjhe jo sukhan ki qadar ko
Nutq ne haivaan se musht-e-khaak ko insaan kiya
Haider Ali Aatish

Baare duniya mein raho gham-zada ya shad raho
Aisa kuchh kar ke chalo yaan ki bahut yaad raho
Mir Taqi Mir

'Mushafi' ham to ye samjhe the ki hoga koi zakhm
Tere dil mein to bahut kaam rafu kaa nikla
Mushafi Ghulam Hamdani

Ham ko maalum hai jannat ki haqeeqat lekin
Dil ke khush rakhne ko 'ghalib' yeh khayaal achchha hai
Mirza Ghalib

Ab ke ham bichhde to kabhi khvaabon mein milen
Jis tarah sukhe hue phool kitabon mein milen
Ahmad Faraz

Ik naam kya likha tira sahil ki ret par
Phir umr bhar hava se meri dushmani rahi
Parveen Shakir

Acknowledgement

I would like to acknowledge the deep debt I owe to Rekhta Foundation for opening the world of Urdu to me. My deep desire to learn and enjoy Urdu would have remained unfulfilled but for the Rekhta Foundation and the Urdu language resources that it has built brick-by-brick over the years. One of the Rekhta Foundation's initiatives is Aamozish, an online Urdu learning platform. It is a dream-come-true for lay persons with zero exposure to Urdu to become proficient in Urdu and partake of the joys and charms of Urdu. The Rekhta Dictionary is arguably the best online dictionary of Urdu and most of the word meanings in this dictionary have been drawn from the Rekhta Dictionary.

Preface

Urdu is a happy amalgamation of many influences down the centuries – primarily the dialects of Hindi like Khari Boli and Braj Bhasha spoken in North India and Persian, Arabic and Turkic spoken by the nobles and soldiers migrating to India since the start of the 11th Century. It has always been the language spoken by the masses and many Urdu words are common to the spoken Hindi of today. The distinction between Hindi and Urdu may well be in the script (Devanagari for Hindi and Nastaliq for Urdu) but the grammar and lexicography of the two languages is common.

Sher-o-shaayari is the most popular genre of Urdu writing and is often the first exposure to the Urdu language for most of us. Who can forget the popular Hindi film songs of yester years based on ghazals which have enthralled generations in South Asia.

One can read shers online or in books, in either Urdu or Hindi or Romanized Urdu (Urdu in English transliteration). However, there is one key hurdle that comes in the way of one's enjoyment of the sher. While many of the Urdu words used in shers are familiar even to those for whom Urdu is not the first language, one comes across one-off words or compound-words the meaning of which is unknown. And that one unfamiliar word robs the entire sher of its magic!

One may encounter an odd offline dictionary which shows Romanized Urdu words with their English meanings but the vast majority of the words in such a dictionary are well-known and so the shaayari-lovers predicament is not solved. Online dictionaries are available but stopping reading the sher midway, going to an online device to search for the meaning of an unfamiliar word and then returning to the sher is an interruption one can do without!

Hence I have compiled 'The Dictionary of Urdu Poetry - For Shaayari Lovers'. It is designed to be a handy guide for lovers of Urdu shers. You can keep it at hand while being immersed in reading the shers in any script or device that you prefer. The moment you encounter an unfamiliar word, just pop open 'The Dictionary of Urdu Poetry - For Shaayari Lovers' and return quickly to the magic of the sher. The Urdu word is transliterated in English and arranged alphabetically for ease of reference, with the word meaning in English. In addition, the Urdu word is transliterated in Hindi since the pronunciation is rendered truer in Hindi. And to whet one's appetite, select shers preface each alphabet section. The meaning of the likely unfamiliar word in the sher follows in the dictionary section.

I am a North Indian exposed to the Hindi spoken by the common man and thus familiar with the Urdu words used in day-to-day conversational Hindi. I learnt the Urdu script a couple of years back and plunged headlong into reading the shers of the Master Shaayars of South Asia from the 1700s upto the modern era in the Urdu script. They have given me hours and hours of unlimited and timeless pleasure.

From my study of over 6000 of the best-known shers of the Master Shaayars I have identified 2500+ words which were unfamiliar to me, and I am sure, unfamiliar to most lovers of Urdu shaayari with little or no formal exposure to Urdu. I hope 'The Dictionary of Urdu Poetry - For Shaayari Lovers' will enable lovers of Urdu Shaayari to enjoy the shers in all their glory, with minimum interruptions due to vocabulary gaps!

Since this book is meant for those passionate about Urdu shaayari, I have avoided using grammatical terms which may be more relevant for serious students of the Urdu language.

Sunil Gupta 'Mustaqil'

A

Piine ko is jahaan main kaun sii mai nahiin magar
Ishq jo baanttaa hai vo aab-e-hayaat aur hai
Shamim Karhani

Samjhenge na agyaar ko agyaar kahaan tak
Kab tak vo mohabbat ko mohabbat na kahenge
Zaheer Dehlvi

Tumhaaraa husn aaraaish tumhaarii saadgii zevar
Tumhen koii zaruurat hii nahiin banne sanvarne kii
Asar Lakhnavi

Ham kisii aur vaqt ke hain asiir
Subh ke shaam ke rahe hii nahiin
Sarfraz Khalid

Aayaa na ek baar ayaadat ko tuu masiih
Sau baar main fareb se biimaar ho chukaa
Ameer Minai

A

***Aab* आब** Water/Sheen/Lustre/Sparkle/Edge of sword

***Aabaa* आबा** Ancestor/Forefather

***Aabaaii* आबाई** Ancestral

***Aab-daar* आब-दार** Brilliant/Polished

***Aab-e-hayaat* आब-ए-हयात** Elixir/Nectar/Water of immortality

***Aabgiin* अबगीना** Goblet/Glass

***Aab-o-giil* आब-ओ-गील** Water and soil

***Aab-o-taab* आब-ओ-ताब** Splendour/Glory/Brilliance

***Aab-juu* आब-जू** Stream/Rivulet/Brook

***Aabruu* आब्रू** Respect/Honour/Chastity/Virginity/Status/Rank/Fame/Credibility/Brightness

***Aadaab* आदाब** Greetings/Salutations/Form of address/Decorum/Politeness/Civility/Elegant manners

***Aadam-e-khaakii* आदम-ए-ख़ाक़ी** Mortal man/Adam made of clay

***Aadil* आदिल** One who acts justly or equitably/One whose testimony is trustworth

***Aafaaq* आफ़ाक़** Horizons/The world

Aafaat **आफ़ात** Calamities

Aafat-talab **आफत-तलब** Calamity seeking

Aafiyat **आफ़ियत** Well-being/Security

Aafriin **आफरीन** Well-begun

Aaftaab **आफ़्ताब** Sun

Aagahii **आगाही** Awareness

Aagaz **आगाज़** Beginning

Aahan **आहन** Iron

Aahang **आहंग** Sound/Voice/Purpose/Method/Rhythm/Harmony/Tune/Melody/Musical composition

Aahuu **आहू** Deer

Aaiin **आईं** Constitution/Manifesto

Aainda **आइंदा** Future

Aajizii **आजिज़ी** Humility

Aakhirat **आख़िरत** Life after death/Hereafter

Aalaa-zarf **आला-ज़र्फ़** Elegance (of manners)/High capacity

Aalam **आलम** World/Condition/Situation

Aalam-e-iijaad **आलम-ए-ईजाद** World of innovation

Aalam-e-vajuud **आलम-ए-वजूद** World of existence

Aalim **आलिम** Doctor

Aalooda **आलूदा** Contaminated/Spoilt/Polluted/Foul/Impure/Unclean/Grimy/Sullied

Aamaadgii **आमादगी** Inclination/Willingness/Readiness/Preparedness

Aamaal **आमाल** Deeds/Conduct/Behaviour

Aamad **आमद** Arrival/Visit/Advent/Income

Aamad-o-shud **आमद-ओ-शुद** Coming and going/Existence

Aamozish **आमोज़िश** Education/Teaching/Learning

Aan **आन** Moment/Dignity/Mode/Manner

***Aaphii* आपही** You only

***Aaraaii* आराई** Embellishment

***Aaraaish* आराइश** Adornment

***Aaraam-e-jaan* आराम-ए-जान** Comfort of life/Beloved/Children (specially son)

***Aarastaa* आरस्ता** Decorated and embellished

***Aarif* आरिफ़** Enlightened/Wise/Knowing/Godly/Pious/Mystic/Sufi/Sage

***Aariyatii* आरियति** Borrowed/Lent/Transient

***Aariz* आरिज़** Cheek

***Aasaab* आसाब** Nerves

***Aasaar* आसार** Indications/Signs/Ruins/Relics

***Aaseb* आसेब** Calamity/Trouble/Madness/Evil spirit/Demon/Illness/Apparition/Ill-fortune/Shock/Pain

***Aaseb-zada* आसेब-ज़दा** Haunted/Ghostly/Under the influence of an evil spirit

***Aashob* आशोब** Crisis/Calamity/Tumult

***Ashob-e-maaash* आशोब-ए-मआश** Economic crisis

***Aashkaar* आशकार** Manifest/Visible

***Aashkaaraa* आशकारा** Clear/Obvious/Manifest/Visible

***Aashnaa-e-hirs* आशना-ए-हिर्स** Knower of greed

***Aashufta* आशुफ़्ता** Distressed

***Aasii* आसी** Sinner

***Aasmaan* आसमान** Firmament/Sky

***Aastaan* आस्तां** Abode

***Aasuuda* आसूदा** Satisfied/Content

***Aatish* आतिश** Anger/Rage/Passion/Fire/Flame/Ignite

Aatishiin **आतिशीं** Fire-like/Passionate/Igneous/Ablaze/Aflame/Fiery/Glowing

Aavaaza-e-jamaal **आवाज़-ए-जमाल** Voice of beauty

Aazmaaish **आज़माइश** Trial/Test/Experiment

Aazurdagii **आज़ुर्दगी** Woe/Grief/Sorrow/Anger/Depression/Displeasure/Dejection/Distress

Abaa **अबा** Cloak/Gown

Abas **अबस** Futile/Purposeless

Abjad **अबजद** Arrangement of 28 letters of the Arabic alphabet, each letter having a numerical value

Abru **अबरू** Eyebrow

Abtaar **अबतार** Dishevelled/Tousled

Abtarii **अब्तरी** Deteriorating/Disorderly/Confusion/Upset/Tired

Adaaegii **अदाएगी** Payment/Settlement

Adaa-fahm **अदा-फ़हम** One who appreciates grace and manners

Adl **अद्ल** Justice/Equity

Adam **अदम** Nonentity/Lack/Want/Life after death/Void/Death

Adaavatein **अदावतें** Enmity

Adeeb **अदीब** Author

Adna **अदना** Trivial/Petty/Insignificant

Afkaar **अफ़्कार** Thoughts/Ideas/Opinions/Theories/Worries

Aflaak **अफ़्लाक** Skies/Heavens

Afshaan **अफ़्शां** Tinsel used by women for make-up

Afshaanii **अफ़्शानी** Dispersal/Scattering/Strewing/Sparkling

Afsurda **अफ़्सुर्दा** Sorry

Afsurdagi **अफ़्सुर्दगी** Depression/Melancholy

Afsuun **अफ़्सूं** Enchantment

***Afzuun* अफ़्ज़ूं** Much greater/Much more

***Agarche* अगरचे** Although/Though/Even if/Granted that

***Agyaar* अग्यार** Strangers/Opponents

***Ahad* अहद** One/Digit one/Unique/God/Having no partner (as an attribute of Allah)

***Aharman* अहरमन** God of badness for Zoroastrians

***Ahbaab* अहबाब** Friend/Lover/Dear ones

***Ahaadis* अहादीस** Anectdotes of companions (of Muhammad)

***Ahd* अह्द** Time/Season/Epoch/Period/Reign/Promise/Vow/Oath

***Ahd-o-paimaan* अह्द-ओ -पैमान** Treaty/Agreement/Unique promise/Vows and promises

***Ahmak* अहमक** Idiot

***Ahvaal* अहवाल** Condition/State/Affairs/Circumstances/Happenings/Events/Situation

***Ahyaa* अह्या** Clans/Tribes/Families/The living

***Ain* ऐन** Real/Exact

***Ain-hijr* ऐन-हिज्र** Exactly like disunion/Separation itself

***Ajal* अजल** Death

***Ajdaad* अजदाद** Ancestors/Forefathers

***Ajiizii* अजीज़ी** Helplessness/Humility/Submissiveness/Inability

***Ajr* अज्र** Pay/Wage/Compensation/Reward for good deeds

***Ajzaa* अज्ज़ा** Particles/Constituents/Ingredients

***Akaarat* अकारत** Fruitless

***Akhlaaq* अख़लाक़** Virtue/Piety/Exemplary behaviour

***Akhtar* अख़्तर** Star

Alaamat **अलामत** Sign/Token/Seal/Stamp/Indication/Symptom/Emblem/Insignia/Standard

Alaav **अलाव** Bonfire

Alam **अलम** Pain/Grief/Affliction/Anguish/Torment

Alast **अलस्त** Wisdom

Alqaab **अलक़ाब** Titles/Honorific names/Form of address in letter writing

Amaa **अमा** Bowels

Amad-o-shud **आमद-ओ-शुद** Comings and goings

Aman-khvaah **अमन-ख़्वाह** Seeker of peace

Ambaar **अम्बार** Heap/Pile/Stack/Hoard/Stock/Collection

Ambariin **अम्बरीन** Amber-like/Of the colour or odour like amber/Fragrant

Amdan **अमदन** Intentionally/Wilfully

Amla **अमला** Staff

Amrad **अमरद** Beardless/Handsome tyouth

Amrad-parast **अमरद-परस्त** Sodomite

Anaadil **अनादिल** Nightingales

Anaasir **अनासिर** Elements

Anal-haq **अनल-हक़** I am God/Truth

Anal-bahar **अनल-बहर** I am ocean

Andaliib **अंदलीब** Nightingale

Andaruun **अन्दरून** Inner/Heart/Internal/The interior/Part of a house reserved for women

Andesha **अंदेशा** Apprehension/Anxiety/Fear/Doubt/Suspicion

Andoh **अन्दोह** Grief/Sorrow/Sorrowful/Full of grief/Torture

Andoh-rubaa **अन्दोह-रुबा** Eliminator of grief

Anfus **अनफ़ूस** Spirituality

***Angbiin* अंगबीन** Honey/ Syrup

***Angusht* अंगुश्त** Finger

***Aniis* अनीस** Companion

***Anjum* अंजुम** Stars

***Anjuman* अंजुमन** Society/ Association

***Anjuman-aaraaiyon* अंजुमन-आराइयों** Parties

***Anqaa* अंक़ा** Very rare/ Unavailable/Extinct/ Mythical bird like phoenix/Woman with long neck

***Anvaar* अनवार** Shining/ Resplendent

***Aqaarib* अक़ारिब** Kith and kin

***Aqd* अक़्द** Treaty/Contract/ Agreement/Wedding/ Marriage knot/Tie

***Aqdas* अक़दस** Sacred

***Aqiida* अक़ीदा** Tenet/ Doctrine/Doctrine of faith or belief

***Aqiidat* अक़ीदत** Attachment/Affection/ Faith/Alliance

***Aqdas* अक़दस Sacred**

***Aqvaam* अक़्वाम** Nations/ Peoples/Races

***Araaish* अराइश** Adornment

***Araq* अरक़** Juice/Essence

***Araq-aaluud* अरक़-आलूद** Perspiring/Sweaty/ Covered with sweat

***Araq-e-infiaal* अरक़-ए-इंफीआल** Beads of perspiration/Sweat of repentance

***Arbaab* अरबाब** Persons/ Masters/Lords/ Possessors/Supporters

***Arkaan* अरकान** Fundamentals

***Arsa-e-hastii* अरसा-ए-हस्ती** Life-time

***Arsh* अर्श** Celestial/Heaven

***Arsh-e-bariin* अर्श-ए-बरीं** The highest heaven

***Arzaan* अरज़ां** Of low value/Cheap

***Arz-o-samaa* अर्ज़-ओ-समां** Earth and sky

***Asaa* असा** Stick/Stave/Support

***Asaasa* असासा** Household property/Wealth/Belongings

***Asbaab* अस्बाब** Justifications/Motives/Worldly goods/Belongings

***Ashad* अशद** Urgent/Exigent

***Ashk-baar* अश्क-बार** Tearful

***Ashuftaghi* आशुफ़्तगी** Distress/Affliction/Perturbation/Distraction/Anxiety/Disorder

***Asiir* असीर** Prosoner

***Asl* अस्ल** Pure/Unadulterated/Real/Legitimate/Pedigree/Principal amount/Actual incident/Standard

***Asr* अस्र** Late afternoon/Time of the day before sunset/Time/Age/Epoch/Era

***Asraar* अस्रार** Secrets/Mysteries/Ghost/Evil spirit/Spectre

***Assasa* असासा** Household property/Belongings/Wealth/

***Ataa* अता** Gift/Concession

***Atfaal* अत्फ़ाल** Children/Offspring

***Atraaf* अतराफ़** Sides/Directions/Around/Suburbs

***Aubaashon* औबाशों** Wanton/Wicked/Licentious/Baddies

***Auj* औज** Light

***Auqaat* औक़ात** Status/Time/Hours/Position/Circumstances/Means/Resources

***Auraad* औराद** Sacred chantings

***Auraaq* औराक़** Petals/Pages

***Ausaaf* औसाफ़** Good qualities

***Ayaadat* अयादत** Enquire about patient's well-being

Ayaan **अयां** Evident/Clear

Ayyaam **अय्याम** Time/Duration/Seasons/Menstrual period/Days

Ayyaar **अय्यार** Artful/Cunning/Crafty/Imposter

Ayyaarii **अय्यारी** Guile/Cunningness/Slyness

Az **अज़** From/Then/By

Azaab **अज़ाब** Torment/Curse/Agony/Anguish/Divine punishment/Troublesome affair/Turbulent/Disorderly

Azaab-e-barq-e-baraan **अज़ाब-ए-बर्क़-ए-बरां** Calamity of lightning and rain

Azaadaaron **अज़ादारों** Mourners

Azal **अज़ल** Eternity/Beginning of time

Az-bas **अज़-बस** Vastly/Very much/Extremely necessary

Az-bas-ki **अज़-बस-कि** That's why

Aziyyat **अज़िय्यत** Trouble/Torment/Difficulty/Torture

Az-khud-rafta **अज़-खुद-रफ्ता** Automatically gone

Azm **अज़्म** Conviction/Determination/Fortitude/Intention

Azmatein **अज़मतें** Majesties

Azm-e-junoon **अज़्म-ए-जुनूं** Determination of frenzy

B

'Jauhar' tumhen nafrat hai bahut baada-kashii se
Barsaat men dekhenge ham inkaar tumhaaraa
Lala Madhav Ram Jauhar

Kchh bataa tuu hii nasheman kaa pataa
main to ai baad-e-sabaa bhuul gayaa
Majrooh Sultanpuri

Ham hain mushtaaq aur vo bezaar
Yaa ilaahii ye maajraa kyaa hai
Mirza Ghalib

Chupke se guzarte hain khabar bhii nahiin hotii
Din raat bhii kam-bakht javaanii kii tarah hain
Azlan Shah

Nayaa bismil huun main vaaqif nahiin rasm-e-shahaadat se
Bataa de tuu hii ai zaalim tadapne kii adaa kyaa hai
Chakbast Brij Narayan

Baab-e-ilm **बाब-ए-इल्म** Chapter/Door of knowledge

Baab-e-iltijaa **बाब-ए-इल्तिजा** Door of requesting or pleading

Baadaa Glass/Goblet

Baada-gulfaam **बादा-गुलफ़ाम** Rose-coloured wine

Baada-kashii **बादा-कशी** Drinking of wine

Baada-nosh **बादा-नोश** Wine drinker

Baadbaan **बादबां** Of or related to sails/Mast

Baad-e-fanaa **बाद-ए-फ़ना** After death

Baad-e-sabaa **बाद-ए-सबा** Morning breeze/Zephyr

Baadiya-paimaaii **बादिया-पैमाई** Wind measurement

Baahamii **बाहमी** Mutual

Baais **बाईस** Cause/Occasion/Basis

Baalaaii-aamdanii **बालाई-आमदनी** Extra income

Baaliidgii **बालीदग़ी** Growth/Development/Vegetation/Loftiness/Maturity/Adolescence

Baam-e-haram **बाम-ए-हरम** Roof of Kaaba

Ba-andaaz **ब-अंदाज़** By way of/According to

Baang-e-jaras **बांग-ए-जरस** Sound of caravan bells

Ba-haq **ब-हक़** True

Baar **बार** Load/Burden

Baaraan **बाराँ** Rains

Baare **बारे** About/In connection with/At last

Baar-e-khaatir **बार-ए-ख़ातिर** Unpleasant/ Disagreeable

Baar-e-nashaat **बार-ए-नशात** Burden/onus of ecstasy/

Baargaah **बारगाह** Audience hall/Court

Baar-haa **बार-हा** Many times

Baar-var **बार-वर** Endure/ To bear fruit

Baatil **बातिल** False/ Untrue/Wrong/ Incorrect/Spurious/ Unreal/Fictitious

Baatin **बातिन** Internal/ Mind/Heart

Baavar **बावर** Confidence

Baaz **बआज़** Few/Some/ Sundry/Diverse

Baaz **बाज़** Refrain/Desist

Baazgasht **बाज़गश्त** Echo/ Return/Restitution/ Restoration/Reaction

Baaziicha **बाज़ीचा** Playground/Toy/Child's play/Fun/Play/Frolic/ Sport

Baaz-pasiin **बाज़-पसीन** Last/Hindmost

Ba-dam **बदम** At the moment

Ba-dastuur **बदस्तूर** As before/As usual/In status quo/Customarily

Bad-gumaan **बद-गुमां** Disloyal/Distrustful

Bad-havaasii **बद-हवासी** Insensitive/Harassed

Badr **बद्र** Full moon/ Accounting mistake

Bad-zan **बद-ज़न** Mistrustful/Suspicious

Ba-gard **ब-गर्द** Around

Baguulaa **बगूला** Whirlwind

Ba-hangaam-e-sahar Time of morning

Bahar **बहर** Without

Bahar-haal **बहर-हाल** At any rate/In any case

Bahar-taur **बहर-तौर** Anyway

Baham **बहम** Along with/ Together

Bahisht **बहिश्त** Heaven

Bahr **बह्र** For/Ocean/In any/By every/To every (way, mean, etc)

Bahr-e-khudaa **बह्र-ए-ख़ुदा** For God's sake

Baht **बह्त** Pure/ Unadulterated/ Unmixed/Only

Baiat **बइअत** Swearing allegiance/Homage/ Fealty

Baiid **बईद** Beyond

Bairuun **बैरूँ** Outside

Bajaa **बजा** Suitable/ Appropriate/Right/ Correct

Ba-jaae **ब-जाए** In place of/ Instead of/In lieu of

Ba-juz **ब-जुज़** Except/ Beside

Bakhiilii **बख़ीली** Avarice/Parsimony/ Niggardliness

Bakhiya-gar **बख़िया-गर** Tailor

Bakht **बख़्त** Destiny/Luck

Bansa-navaaz **बंसा -नवाज़** Lord/God/Sir/Patron/ One who takes care of someone

Bapaa **बपा** In progress/ Going on/Afoot

Baqaa **बक़ा** Perpetuity/ Permanence/Eternity

Ba-qadr **ब-क़द्र** Appreciate

Ba-qaul **ब-क़ौल** According to

Bar **बर** Bear fruit/Land

Barahana **बरहना** Nude/ Naked/Uncovered/Bare

Barahnagii **बरहनगी** Nudity

Bar-aks **बर-अक्स** On the contrary/As against/In opposition(to)

Barg **बर्ग** Leaf

Bargashta **बर्गश्ता** Angry/ Upset/Turned back/ Changed

Barg-e-gul **बर्ग-ए-गुल** Leaf of flower/Rose petal

Barham **बरहम** Angry/ Vexed/Inflamed

***Barhamii* बरहमी** Confusion/Anarchy/Anger/Vexation/Displeasure/Trouble/Wrath

***Barhana-paa* बरहना-पा** Bare feet

***Bar-khud-galat* बर-ख़ुद-ग़लत** Self-mistake

***Barpaa* बरपा** Happen

***Barq-paaron* बर्क़-पारों** Shards/pieces of lightning

***Barsar* बर्सर** On/In

***Ba-tadbiir* ब-तदबीर** By strategy

***Bartarii* बरतरी** Excellence/Eminence/Superiority/Ascendancy/Altitude

***Bar-waqt* बर-वक़्त** Opportune

***Bashaarat* बशारत** Good news/Glad tidings/Revelation

***Bashar* बशर** Man/Human being

***Bashariiyat* बशरीयत** Human beings

***Basiirat* बसीरत** Sight/Insight/Foresight/Prudence/Knowledge/Understanding/Intelligence/Discernment

***Baski* बस्कि** Although

***Bast-e-zulf* बस्त-ए-ज़ुल्फ़** Hair tied

***Basyaar* बसयार** Many/Much/Multitudinous

***Ba-tang* ब-तंग** Distressed/Vexed/In dire straits

***Ba-vaqt* ब-वक़्त** At the time

***Bayaabaan* बयाबाँ** Wilderness/Desert

***Bayaabaanon* बयाबानों** Wilderness (p)

***Bayaaz* बयाज़** book in which poet writes verse/Account book

***Ba-zaahir* ब-ज़ाहिर** Apparently/Outwardly/Ostensibly/Externally/In appearance

Bazm-e-suruur Party of esctasy

Be-ahaadiis **बे-अहादीस** Without traditions or anecdotes of companions of Prophet Mohammad

Be-baak **बे-बाक़** Fearless

Be-bahra **बे-बहरा** Deprived of benefit/Unlucky/Poor

Bedaad **बेदाद** Injustice/Tyranny/Oppression/Violence

Bedaar **बेदार** Awakened

Be-gaana **बे-गाना** Strange/Unconcerned/Not related/Estranged/Foreign/Alien/Exotic

Begaana-var **बेगाना-वर** Like a stranger or alien/Apathetic/Without enthusiasm

Be-haiat **बे-हैअत** Amorphous/Unshaped/Shapeless/Formless/Unformed

Be-his **बे-हिस** Insensitive

Be-huzuur **बे-हुज़ूर** Absent/Not present/Non-existent/Disgraceful

Bejaa **बेजा** Improper/Misplaced/Unlawful/Beyond limit/Wrongly/Improperly

Be-kaifii **बे-कैफ़ी** Dull/Drab/Insipid/Uninteresting

Bekalii **बेक़ाली** Restlessness

Be-kanaar **बे-कनार** Boundless/Without a shore/Infinite

Be-karaan **बे-करां** Limitless/Boundless/Immense/Unbounded/Shoreless

Be-kas **बे-कस** Helpless

Be-khatar **बे-ख़तर** Free from danger/Fearlessly/Safe

Be-muravvat **बे-मुरव्वत** Unkind/Uncivil/Inhuman

Be-naqat **बे-नकत** Without using diacritical dots

Be-navaa **बे-नवा** Destitute/Indigent

Be-naziir **बे-नज़ीर** Matchless/Unique/Peerless

Be-niyaazaanaa **बे-नियाज़ाना** Careless

Be-niyaaz **बे-नियाज़** Carefree/Independent/Without want

Be-niyaazi **बे-नियाज़ी** Aloofness/Air of carelessness/Without want/Carefree

Be-paayaan **बे-पायां** Immeasurable

Be-panaah **बे-पनाह** Without shelter

Be-parha **बे-परहा** Deprived of benefit

Be-par-o-baalii **बे-पर-ओ-बाली** State of being without wings and hair/Helplessness/Compulsion

Be-qasd **बे-क़स्द** Unintended

Be-rabt **बे-रब्त** Disjointed/Disonnected/Unrelated/Irrelevant/Unconnected

Be-ridaaii **बे-रिदाई** Without a shawl/scarf/covering

Be-saakhta **बे-साख़्ता** Spontaneously/Extempore

Be-sabaat **बे-सबात** Mortal/Transitory

Be-sar-o-saamaaniyon **बे-सर-ओ-सामानियों** Homeless

Beshtar **बेश्तर** For the most part/Mostly/Generally/Often

Be-suruur **बे-सुरूर** Without ecstasy

Be-suud **बे-सूद** Useless

Be-zaar **बे-ज़ार** Bored

Be-zaarii **बे-ज़ारी** Boredom/Unhappiness/Displeasure/Disgust/Annoying

Be-zarii **बे-ज़री** Poverty

Bhaan-bhod **भान-भोड़** Tear and mangle

Bharam **भरम** Reputation/Trust/Secret

Biim **बीम** Despair

Biinaaii **बीनाई** Eyesight/Vision

Biinash **बीनाश** Vision

***Billa* बिला** Without

***Binaa* बिना** Basis

***Bint* बिन्त** Daughter

***Bint-ul-inab* बिन्त-उल-इनाब** Daughter of grape/wine

***Birog* बिरोग** Separation from beloved

***Bisaat* बिसात** Capacity/Power/Bedding/Carpet/Chess-board

***Bismil* बिस्मिल** Slaughtered animal/Afflicted lover

***Bosiida* बोसीदा** Rotten/Decayed

***Bos-o-kanaar* बोस-ओ-कनार** Kissing and fondling/Dalliance/To do love

***Bul-havas* बुल-हवस** Very greedy

***Buud* बूद** Existence/Being/Happened/Was

***Buud-o-baash* बूद-ओ-बाश** Whereabouts/Way of life/Manner of living/Subsistence/(Metaphorically) Abode/Residence/Existence

***Buu-qalamoon* बू-क़लमून** Variegated/Diversity

C

Koii chaaraa nahiin duaa ke sivaa
Koii suntaa nahiin khudaa ke sivaa
Hafeez Jalandhari

Hogii na chaaraagar tirii tadbiir kaargar
Ham ko khud apne zakhmon kii chaahat hai aaj-kal
Ameer Nehtauri

Aao to mere sahn men ho jaae raushnii
muddat guzar gaii hai charaagaan kiye hue
Ashhad Bilal Ibn-E-Chaman

Dil vo kaafir hai ki mujh ko na diyaa chiin kabhii
Bevafaa tuu bhii use le ke pashemaan hogaa
Bekhud Dehlvi

Na chitvan aap kii thahrii na dil miraa thahraa
Use sukuun ho to is ko bhii kuchh qaraar rahe
Ashique Akbarabadi

C

***Chaao-chuuz* चाओ-चूज़** Dalliance/Fondness/ Gratifying every wish/ Caressing

***Chaara* चारा** Remedy/ Option/Way

***Chaaraagar* चारागर** Doctor

***Chaar-girah* चार-गिरह** Four knors/Span

***Chakiidan* चकीदन** Throw

***Champaii* चम्पई** Light yellow colour

***Charaagaan* चारागां** Display of lights/ Illumination/ Illuminating of lamps

***Charkh* चर्ख** Sky/Celestial orb/Potter's wheel/ Carousel/Hyaena/ Fortune/Destiny

***Chashma-e-aab-e-hayaat* चश्म-ए-आब-ए-हयात** Fountain of immortality

***Chiin* चीन** Wrinkle/Frown

***Chitvan* चितवन** Appearance/Look/ Glance/The state of seeing someone with love and affection

***Chob* चोब** Wood/Stick

D

Tum jo chaaho to mire dard kaa darmaan ho jaae
Varna mushkil hai ki mushkil mirii aasaan ho jaae
Bedam Shah Warsi

Dasht jaisii ujaad hain ankhen
In dariichon se khvaab kyaa jhaanken
Siraj Faisal Khan

Ham ajnabii hain aaj bhii apne dayaar men
Har shakhs puuchhtaa hai yahii tum yahaan kahaan
Waheeda Naseem

Uthe jaate hain diida-var sabhii aahista aahista
Ye duniyaa mo'tabar logon se khaalii hotii jaatii hai
Ateeq Asar

Vo hii aasaan karegaa mirii dushvaarii ko
Jis ne dushvaar kiyaa hai mirii aasaanii ko
Parveen Umm-E-Mushtaq

***Daad* दाद** Praise/Applause

***Daag-e-alam* दाग-ए-अलम** Spot of tragedy

***Daaim* दाइम** Perpetual/ Eternal/Continuing always/Lasting/ Perpetually/ Continuously/ Permanent

***Daalaan* दालान** Vestibule/ Covered way/Corridor/ Yard/Lobby

***Daam* दाम** Snare/Bait/ Trap/Chain

***Daamaan* दामान** Foot of hill/Skirt/Part of garment below chest/ Refuge/Protection/ Peace

***Daamaan-e-falak* दामान-ए-फ़लक** Expanse of sky

***Daaman-giir* दामन-गीर** Attached (to)/Adherent/ Dependant/Claimant/ Accuser/Plaintiff/ Seeking redress(from)

***Daam-e-ajal* दाम-ए-अजल** Clutches of death

***Daaman-kashaan* दामन-काशां** Walking with dignity and grace/Dragging or trailing the skirt/ Turning away (from)/ Abandoning/Shunning

***Daanaa* दाना** Sage/Wise man/Wise/Learned/ Wise/Prudent

***Daanaaii* दानाई** Wisdom

***Daang* दांग** Direction

***Daanista* दानिस्ता** Knowingly/Wittingly/ Deliberately

***Daar* दार** Gallows

***Daar-e-faanii* दार-ए-फ़ानी** House of mortality

***Daavar* दावर** Judge

***Daavar-e-mahashar* दावर-ए- महशर** Judge on judgement day

***Dabiiz* दबीज़** Coarse/Thick

***Dabistaan* दबिस्तां** School/ School of thought

***Dafatan* दफ़अतन** Suddenly

***Dafiina* दफ़ीना** Hidden treasure

***Dahaan* दहन** Mouth

***Dahqaan* दहक़ां** Farmer/ Peasant

***Dahr* दहर** World/Era/ Time/Period

***Dakhal* दख़ल** Occupancy/ Occupation/Possession

***Dakhiil* दख़ील** Intruder/ Invader

***Dalak* दलक** Trembling/ Shaking/Tottering/ Quaking/Vibration/ Shock/Blow

***Dam* दाम** Trap/Price/Cost

***Damaadam* दमादम** Repetitive/Rhythmic/ Continuously/Frantically leaping & making noise in a fit of esctasy

***Dam-ba-dam* दम-ब-दम** Continuously/ Constantly/Incessantly/ In every moment/ Repeatedly

***Dam-e-naza* दम-ए-नज़ा** Time of death

***Dam-e-tahriir* दम-ए-तहरीर** Time of writing

***Danish* दानिश** Knowledge/ Learning/Wisdom

***Danish-e-hazir* दानिश-ए-हाज़िर** Contemporary knowledge

***Daraa* दरा** Caravan bells

***Daraaz* दराज़** Long/High/ Exalted

***Darakhshaan* दरख़्शां** Shining/Brilliant/ Resplendent

***Darakht* दरख़्त** Tree

***Dardmand* दर्दमंद** Sympathiser/Friend

***Dar-guzar* दर-गुज़र** Overlook/Pass by/Turn aside (from)/Neglect

***Dar-haqeeqat* दर-हक़ीक़त** Matter of fact/In fact

***Dariida* दरीदा** Torn/Rent/Ragged/Tired/Upset

***Dariya-nosh* दरिया-नोश** Excessive drinker

***Darke* दरके** Damaged

***Darmaan* दरमान** Medicine/Remedy/Cure/Solution

***Dar-parda* दर-पर्दा** Concealed/Veiled/Hidden/Secret/Privately

***Darpesh* दरपेश** Under consideration/Placed before

***Dars* दर्स** Lesson/Lecture

***Daruud* दरुद** Praise of Prophet Mohammad

***Daruun* दरूं** Inside

***Daryaaft* दरयाफ़्त** Discovery

***Dashnaa* दशना** Dagger

***Dasht* दश्त** Forest

***Dasht-e-laa-makaan* दश्त-ए- ला-मकान** Infinite desert

***Dasht-navardii* दश्त-ए-नवर्दी** Wandering in the desert

***Dastaar* दस्तार** Turban

***Dastaras* दस्तरस** Reach/Access/Within one's power/Ability/Power

***Dastar-khvaan* दस्तर-ख्वां** Piece of cloth spread on the ground on which food is served

***Dast-ba-dast* दस्त-ब-दस्त** Hand to hand/Quickly/Hand to had (fight)/Back to back/Facr to face

***Dast-basta* दस्त-बस्ता** Humbly/Respectfully/With folded hands

***Dast-e-aduu* दस्त-ए-अदू** Enemy's hand

***Dast-e-chup* दस्त-ए-चुप** Left hand

***Dast-e-daadaar* दस्त-ए-दादर** Hand of the creator

Dast-e-ras **दस्त-ए-रस** Right hand

Dast-nigar **दस्त-निग़र** Needy/In need of

Daulat-e-sar **दौलत-ए-सर** Wealth of the mind

Daulat-e-faqr-o-fanaa **दौलत-ए-फ़क्र-ओ-फ़ना** Weakth of asceticism

Daur-e-daamaan **दौर-ए-दामां** Time/period of peace/protection/refuge

Dayaar **दयार** Territory/ Region

Dhaaras **धारस** Consolation

Dhanak **धनक** Rainbow

Dhaulaa **धौला** White/ Clear/Bright/Any white thing/White colour

Digar **दिगर** Other

Diida-e-hairaan **दीदा-ए-हैरां** Discerning eyes

Diida-e-khuun-baar **दीदा-ए- ख़ून-बार** Weeping with or due to extreme pain

Diidanii **दीदानी** Worth seeing

Diida-var **दीदा-वर** Sharp-sighted/Perspicacious/ Visionary/Perceptive

Diigar **दीग़र** Other/ Another/Once more/ Again

Diivaar-e-tarab **दीवार-ए-तरब** Wall of joy, delight, happiness

Dil-afgaar **दिल-अफ्ग़ार** Heart-broken/ Degected/Melancholy/

Dil-e-aagaah **दिल-ए-आगाह** Prudent/Vigilant

Dil-e-naa-kardaa-kaar **दिल-ए-ना-करदा-गार** Heart whose efforts are futile

Dil-fareb **दिल-फ़रेब** Heart-alluring/Enticing/ Charming

Dil-giir **दिल-गीर** Sad/ Melancholy

Dil-juu **दिल-जू** Searcher of heart/One who gives solace

Dil-navaaz **दिल-नवाज़** Kind/Benevolent

***Dil-shikan* दिल-शिकन**
Heart-breaking

***Divaana-var* दीवाना-वर**
With frenzy

***Dil-zada* दिल-ज़दा**
Wounded or stricken to the heart/Wounded

***Diraa* दिरा** Insight

***Do-aalam* दो-आलम**
Universe/Both worlds

***Doshiizgii* दोशीज़गी**
Virginity/Maidenhood

***Durd-e-tah-e-jaam* दुर्द-ए-तह-ए-जाम** Dregs or sediment at the bottom of a glass of wine

***Dur-e-nayaab* दुर-ए-नायाब**
Rare pearl

***Dushvaarii* दुश्वारी** Difficulty

***Duud* दूद** Smoke/Haze/Mist/Vapour

***Duur-as-tariiq* दूर-ए-तरीक़**
Atheist/Iniquity

***Duzdeeda* दुज़दीदा** A furtive glance/By stealth/Clandestinely/Sly/Stolen/Purloined/Pilfered/

***Duzd-e-hinaa* दुज़्द-ए-हिना**White spaces left in the hand after application of henna

E

Chal to saktaa thaa main bhii paanii par
Main ne dariyaa kaa ehtiraam kiyaa
Anjum Saleemi

Safar pe nikle hain ham puure ehtimaam ke saath
Ham apne ghar se kafan saath le ke aae hain
Iqbal Azeem

Rishton kaa etibaar vafaaon kaa intizaar
Ham bhii charaag le ke havaaon men aae hain
Nida Fazli

Mohabbaten to faqat intihaaen maangtii hain
Mohabbaton men bhalaa etidaal kyaa karnaa
Hasan Abbas Raza

Main jurm kaa etiraaf kar ke
Kuchh aur hai jo chhupaa gayaa huun
Jaun Eliya

E

Eajaaz **एअजाज़** Miracle

Eazaaz **एअज़ाज़** Honour/ Respect

Ehtaraam **एहतराम** Respect

Ehtimaam **एहतिमाम** Preparation/Planning/ Care

Ehtiraaz **एहतिराज़** To avoid/Guarding against/ Abstaining from/ Being cautious of/ Abstinence/Avoidance

Etibaar **ऐतिबार** Trust/ Belief/Respect/Regard/ Credence/Faith/ Credibiity/Esteem

Etibaaraat **एतिबारात** Reliance/Trusts

Etidaal **ऐतिदाल** Moderation

Etiqaad **ऐतिक़ाद** Conviction/Religious belief

Etiraaf **ऐतिराफ़** Admission/Confession/ Agree

F

Jo rang-e-ishq se faarig ho us ko dil nahiin kahte
Jo maujon se na takraae use saahil nahiin kahte
Wasif Dehlvi

Ab kar ke faraamosh to naashaad karoge
Par ham jo na honge to bahut yaad karoge
Meer Taqi Meer

Ham ishq men hain fard to tum husn men yaktaa
Ham saa bhii nahiin ek jo tum saa nahiin koii
Lala Madhav Ram Jauhar

Kyuun na firdaus men dozakh ko milaa len yaarab
Sair ke vaaste thodii sii jagah aur sahii
Mirza Ghalib

Khamoshii dil ko hai furqat men din raat
Ghadii rahtii hai ye aathon pahar band
Lala Madhav Ram Jauhar

Faakhta **फ़ाख़्ता** Dove

Faanii **फ़ानी** Mortal/Perishable/Transitory

Faanuus **फ़ानूस** Chandelier

Faaqa **फ़ाक़ा** Fasting/Starvation/Poverty/Penury

Faaqa-kashii **फ़ाक़ा-क़शी** Starvation

Faaqa-masti **फ़ाक़ा-मस्ती** Cheerfulness in adversity

Faaqon **फ़ाकों** Poverty/Want/Fast

Faarig **फ़ारिग़** Free/Unoccupied/Disengaged/Discharged

Faatah-e-aalam **फ़तह-ए-आलम** Conqueror of world

Faatiha **फ़ातिहा** Opening chapter of Quran/Commencement/First part/Prayers for the dead

Fahm **फ़हम** Understanding/Comprehension/One who understands

Fahmi **फ़हमी** Understanding

Fahrist **फ़हरिस्त** List

Faiz **फ़ैज़** Success/Grace/Favour

Faizaan **फ़ैज़ान** Grace/Beneficence/Good influence

Faiz-yaab **फैज़-याब** Benefitted/Blessed in life

Falak-bos **फ़लक़-बोस** Kissing the sky

***Falak-e-duun* फ़लक़-ए-दूं** Ill-fate/Lower sky

***Falak-e-siflaa* फ़लक़-ए-सिफ़ला** Ignoble or sordid fortune

***Fanaa* फ़ना** Death

***Faqiih* फ़क़ीह** Theologian

***Faqr* फ़क़्र** Poverty

***Faraag* फ़राग़** Leisure/Repose

***Faraagat* फ़राग़त** Cessation from labour/Time for rest/Comfort

***Faraaham* फ़राहम** Amassed/Gathered/Collected/Accumulated/Available/Obtained

***Faraakh* फ़राख़** Ample/Spacious

***Faraakhi* फ़राख़ी** Generosity

***Faraamosh* फ़रामोश** Forgetful

***Faraasiis* फरांसीस** Of or belonging to France/French

***Faraavaan* फ़रावां** Abundant/Ample/Plenty/Copipus/Excess

***Faraaz* फ़राज़** Height/Elevation/High/Elevated

***Farang* फ़रंग** European

***Fard* फ़र्द** Unique/Single/Unmatched/List/Catalogue

***Fardaa* फ़र्दा** Tomorrow

***Farhat* फ़रहत** Pleasure/Happy/Cheerful/Joy/Pleasuring

***Farmaan-ravaa* फ़रमान-रवा** Ruler/Sovereign/One entitled to rule

***Farog* फ़रोग़** Splendour

***Farsang* फ़रसंग** League (3.75 miles)

***Farsuuda* फ़रसूदा** Weathered/Eroded/Spoilt by time or age/Effaced/Outmoded/Worn-out

***Fashaar* फ़शार** Defuse

***Fasiil* फ़सील** Boundary

***Fasurda* फ़सुर्दा** Disappointed/Old/Sad/ Worn-out

***Faut* फ़ौत** Death/Passing away/Expire/Escaping/ Being lost

***Fazaa* फ़ज़ा** Ambience

***Fikr-e-jamiil* फ़िक्र-ए-जमील** Beautiful ideas or thoughts

***Fil-haqeeqat* फिल-हक़ीक़त** Indeed

***Finjaan* फिंजां** Cup for drinking qahwa

***Firdaus* फ़िर्दौस** Paradise/ Garden

***Firqa* फ़िर्क़ा** Sect/ Community/Religious sect or cult/Grou of persons with similar belief

***Firqa-bandii* फ़िर्क़ा-बंदी** Organisation of people into sects/castes/ polarization

***Fishaar* फ़िशार** Pressing or squeezing/Pressure

***Fitna* फ़ित्ना** Temptation/ Mutiny/Revolt/ Discord/Conflict/ Anarchy

***Fitraak* फ़ित्राक** Saddle straps/Cords fixed to a saddle for hanging game from

***Fiza* फ़िज़ा** Space/Air space/Atmosphere

***Fugaan* फ़ुगां** Cry of distress/Lamentation/ Wail/Clamour

***Fuqaraa* फ़ुक़रा** Beggar/ Mystic/Sufi

***Furqat* फ़ुर्क़त** Separation (of lovers)/Absence (of friend or beloved)

***Fusuun* फ़ुसूँ** Enchantment/ Sorcery/Magic/Spell/ Incantation

***Fuzuun* फ़ुज़ून** Many/ Plenty/Increasing

G

Sair kar duniyaa kii gaafil zindagaanii phir kahaan
Zindagii gar kuchh rahii to ye javaanii phir kahaan
Khwaja Meer Dard

Raat din gardish men hain saat aasmaan
Ho rahegaa kuchh na kuchh ghabraaen kyaa
Mirza Ghalib

Ham dard ke maare hii giraan-jaan hain vagarna
Jiinaa tirii furqat men kuchh aasaan to nahiin hai
Azeem Murtaza

Rahii na taaqat-e-guftaar aur agar ho bhii
To kis umiid pe kahiye ki aarzuu kyaa hai
Mirza Ghalib

Phuul barse kahiin shabnam kahiin gauhar barse
Aur is dil kii taraf barse to patthar barse
Bashir Badr

G

***Gaaebaana* ग़ायबाना** Absence/Secretly/Invisibly

***Gaafil* ग़ाफ़िल** Inattentive/Neglectful/Unmindful/Sound asleep/Unconscious/Oblivious (to)

***Gaah* गाह** Sometimes

***Gaalib* ग़ालिब** Superior/Higher/Victorious/Predominant

***Gaalibaan* ग़ालिबां** Probably

***Gaam* ग़ाम** Footstep/Step/Pace (of horse)

***Gaamii* ग़ामी** Steps/Pace/Foot/Accompanying/Companion

***Gaarat* ग़ारत** Destruction/Pillage/Plunder/Ravage

***Gaaza* ग़ाज़ा** Red powder as rouge

***Gab-gab* ग़ब-ग़ब** Double chin

***Gabr* ग़ब्र** Infidel/Pagan/Fire-worshipper/Zorastrian

***Gadaa* ग़दा** Beggar/Mendicant

***Gadaagar* ग़दाग़र** Beggar/Mendicant

***Gadaaii* ग़दाई** Begging/Beggary/Poverty/Mean/Misery/Wretched/Insignificant

***Gadlaa* ग़दला** Dirty/Turbid/Muddy/Foul/Soiled/Heavy

***Gah* गह** House

***Gahe* गाहे** Often/Sometimes/Occasionally

***Gahnaae* गहनाए** Eclipsed

***Gaib* ग़ैब** That which is hidden/mysterious/unseen/Divine

***Gairat* ग़ैरत** Self-respect/Honour/Shame/Modesty/Dignity

***Galiiz* ग़लीज़** Dirty/Filthy/Faeces/Stool

***Gam-gusaar* ग़म-गुसार** Comforter/Consoler

***Gam-kadaa* ग़म-क़दा** Abode of sorrow/mourning

***Gam-khvaar* ग़म-ख़्वार** Sympathiser/Consoler/Comforter/Sympathetic

***Gamnaak* ग़मनाक** Tragic

***Gamza* ग़म्ज़ा** Coquetry/Amorous Glance/Wink

***Gam-zada* ग़म-ज़दा** Afflicted/Aggrieved

***Gandum* गंदुम** Wheat

***Ganiimat* ग़नीमत** Blessing/Boon

***Ganjiina* गन्जीना** Repository/Treasury/Wealth/Granary/Compilation/Store/Magazine

***Garaaben* गराबें** Curved part of the edge of a sword or axe/Crows or ravens

***Garaan* गरां** Unpleasant/Dear/Costly

***Garaz* ग़रज़** Intention/Object/Purpose/End

***Garche* गर्चे** Although/Even/If

***Gardan-zadanii* गर्दन-ज़दनी** Deserve to be beheaded

***Gardish* ग़र्दिश** Revolution/Change of fortune/Vicissitudes

***Gardish-e-ayyaam* ग़र्दिश-ए-अय्यां** Vicissitudes of fortune

***Gardish-e-prakaar* ग़र्दिश-ए-प्रक़ार** Motion of compass

***Garduun* गर्दूं** Sky/Heavens/Firmament

***Gariibaan-e-chaman* गरीबां-ए-चमन** Exiled from one's country

***Gariib-ul-vatan* ग़रीब-उल-वतन** Foreigner

***Garm-e-tavaaf* गर्म-ए-तवाफ़** Eager to circuambulate

***Garq* ग़र्क़** Drowned/ Obsessed

***Garq-e-dariyaa-e-muhiit* ग़र्क़-ए-दरिया-ए-मुहीत** Drowned in encircled river

***Garqaab* ग़र्क़ाब** Drowned

***Garqaabii* ग़र्क़ाबी** Drowning

***Gash* ग़श** Fainting/Stupor

***Gazal-saraa* ग़ज़ल-सरा** One who reads or recites gazals

***Gazal-saraaii* ग़ज़ल-सराई** Reading/reciting/singing Gazal

***Gaziida* ग़ज़ीदा** Injured

***Ghaag* घाघ** Wily/Sly/ Seasoned/Veteran/ Experienced

***Giibat* ग़ीबत** Speaking ill of someone behind his back

***Gil* गिल** Soil

***Gilaurii* गिलौरी** Paan/Betel leaf

***Giraan* गिरां** Weight/ Burden/Grief/ Unpleasant/Expensive

***Giraanbaarii* गिरांबारी** Hardship

***Giraanii* गिरानी** Heavier/ Weighty/Dearness

***Giraan-maaya* गिरां -माया** Exquisite/Precious

***Girafta-dil* गिरफ़्ता-दिल** Sad

***Girah* गिरह** Knot/Joint/ Tie

***Girdaab* ग़िर्दाब** Vortex/ Whirlpool

***Girya* ग़िर्या** Weeping/ Lamentation/Crying/ Tears

***Giryaan* गिरयां** Wailing/ Crying

***Giryaan-naak* गिरयां-नाक़** Weeping/In tears

***Gor* गोर** Tomb

***Gor-e-gariibaan* गोर-ए-गरीबां** Burial ground for poor/strangers

***Gosh* गोश** Ear

***Goshe* गोशे** Corners

***Gubaar-e-dil* ग़ुबार-ए-दिल** Trouble of mind/ Vexation/Displeasure/ Affliction/Harboured bitterness/Resentment

***Gudaaz* गुदाज़** Molten/ Dissolved/Melted/ Softness/Tenderness

***Gufta-e-Ghalib* गुफ़्ता-ए-ग़ालिब** Said by Ghalib

***Guftaar* ग़ुफ़्तार** Speaking/ Telling/Speech/ Conversation

***Gauhar* गौहर** Gem/Pearl/ Sharpness of sword/ Descent/Origin

***Gul-afshaanii* गुल-अफ़शानी** Showering of flowers/Eloquence

***Gul-andaam* गुल-अंदाम** Flower-limbed/Slender/ Delicate

***Gulchiin* गुलचीं** Florist/ Flower gatherer/ Gardener

***Gul-e-tar* गुल-ए-तर** Fresh flower/Beloved with beautiful face

***Gulfaam* गुलफ़ाम** Red/ Rosy/Delicate/Beautiful

***Gul-gasht-e-chaman* गुल-गश्त-ए-चमन** Walk in the garden

***Gulguun* गुलगूं** Rose-coloured/Red-coloured

***Gul-karii* गुल-कारी** Flower painting/Tapestry

***Guluu* गुलू** Throat

***Gumaan* गुमां** Surmise/ Conjecture

***Gum-gashta* गुम-गश्ता** Lost/Missing

***Guncha-lab* गुंचा-लब** Bud of lips/One with a mouth like a bud

***Gurbat* ग़ुर्बत** Poverty

***Gurez* गुरेज़** Escape/ Evasion/Avoid/Run away

***Gurezaan* गुरेज़ां** Fleeing/ Run away from/Escape from

***Guruub* गुरूब** Setting (of sun/moon)/Sunset

***Gusl* ग़ुस्ल** Complete purificatory washing of the whole person/ Bathing/Ablutions

***Gustaakhii* गुस्ताख़ी** Arrogance/ Presumptousness/ Rudeness/Insolence

***Guun* गूँ** Merit

***Guzar-auqaat* गुज़र-औक़ात** Livelihood/ Sustinence

H

Ilaaj kii nahiin haajat dil-o-jigar ke liye
Bas ik nazar tirii kaafii hai umr-bhar ke liye
Munawwr Badayuni

Abhii chhutii nahiin jannat kii dhuul paanv se
Hanuuz farsh-e-zamiin par nayaa nayaa huun main
Iftikhar Mughal

Hadaf bhii mujh ko banaanaa hai aur mere hariif
Mujhii se tiir mujhii se kamaan maangte hain
Manzoor Hashmi

Ik umr sunaaen to hikaayat na ho puurii
Do roz men ham par jo yahaan biit gaii hai
Habib Jalib

Ab in huduud men laayaa hai intizaar mujhe
Vo aa bhii jaaen to aae na etibaar mujhe
Khumar Barabankavi

H

Haa-e-duur-daraaz **हा-ए-दूर-दराज़** Far-reaching

Haail **हाईल** Impediment/Obstacle/Preventing/Hindering

Haajat **हाजत** Necessity/Need/Requirement

Haakim **हाक़िम** Ruler/Judge/Master/Chief

Haasil **हासिल** Gain/Result/Profit/Outcome/Revenue/Result

Habaab **हबाब** Bubble

Hadaf **हदफ़** Target

Hadd-e-nazar **हद्द-ए-नज़र** Line of sight/FHorizon/As far as the eye can see

Hadiya **हादिया** Gift/Present/Conclusion ceremony of Quran where parent gives teacher a gift

Hafiz **हाफ़िज़** Keeper/Guardian/Protector/One who memorizes the Quran

Hafiza **हाफ़िज़ा** Good memory

Haif **हैफ़** Alas/Ah/Pity

Haihaat **हायेहात** Alas/Woe to me/Begone

Haivaan **हैवान** Eternity

Hamal **हमल** Pregnancy

Hajv **हज्व** Lampoon/Satire/Reproach

Hajv-e-mai **हज्व-ए-मये** Seeming praise but lampooning wine

Halaak **हलाक़** Destruction

***Halaavat* हलावट** Sweetness/ Deliciousness/Comfort/ Relief/Relish taste

***Halal* हलल** Legitimate/ right

***Halq* हल्क़** Wind pipe/ Gullet/Throat

***Halqa* हल्क़ा** Links (of a chain)

***Ham-aahangii* हम-आहंगी** Agreement/Harmony/ Concord

***Ham-asron* हम-अस्रों** Contemporaries

***Ham-damon* हम-दमों** Sympathisers

***Ham-safiiron* हम-सफ़ीरों** Whistlers

***Hama-tan-chashm* हमा-तन-चश्म** All eyes

***Hama-tan-gosh* हमा-तन-गोश** All ears

***Ham-kalaam* हम-कलाम** Conversing together

***Ham-kanaar* हम-कनार** Embracing

***Ham-navaa* हम-नवा** Singing in unison/ Friend/Companion

***Ham-raaz* हम-राज़** Confidant/Secret holder

***Ham-safiir* हम-सफ़ीर** Companion/Friend

***Hamvaar* हम-वार** Even/ Level/Smooth/ Consistent/Equable/ Seamless

***Ham-zaad* हम-ज़ाद** Alter ego

***Hangaama-e-hastii* हंगामा-ए-हस्ती** Chaos of life

***Hanuuz* हनूज़** Yet

***Haq* हक़** Truth/Right/ Favour/Due/Claim

***Haqaaeq* हक़ायक़** Facts/ Reality

***Haq-biin* हक़-बीं** Truth-seeker

***Hakiiqat-e-muntazar* हक़ीक़त-ए-मुंतज़र** Awaiting reality/The hereafter

***Haqiir* हक़ीर** Despicable/ Contemptible/Vile/ Mean/Insignificant/ Abject/Base/Least

***Haq-go* हक़-गो** One who speaks for justice

***Haq-goii* हक़-गोई** Telling truth

***Haraarat* हरारत** Fever/ Heat/Warmth/Ardour

***Haram-e-paak* हरम-ए-पाक** Holy mosque

***Harbaa* हर्बा** Arms/ Weapons

***Har-chand* हर-चंद** However/Although/ How-so-ever

***Harf* हर्फ़** Word

***Harf-e-mukarrar* हर्फ़-ए-मुक़र्रर** Repeated word

***Hariif* हरीफ़** Rival/ Opponent/Competitor/ Peer/Mate/Audacious/ Impudent/Clever/ Cunning

***Hariim* हरीम** House/Part of the house reserved for women/Sanctuary/ Walls of Kaaba

***Hariis* हरीस** Greedy/ Covetous/Avaricious/ Greedy or covetous person

***Har-suu* हर-सू** In all directions

***Hasb-e-aarzuu* हज़्ब-ए-आरज़ू** According to wish

***Has-e-rozgaar* हस-ए-रोज़गार** Mundane life

***Hashmat* हश्मत** Dignity/ Pomp/Parade/Riches/ Wealth

***Hashr* हश्र** Tumult/ Commotion/ Lamentation/Wailing/ Gathering/Congregation/ Doomsday/Day of judgement

***Hasratein* हसरतें** Unfulfilled desires/ Regret/Grief/Intense sorrow

***Hast-o-buud* हस्त-ओ-बूद** What is and what was/ All that is or was/The present and past

***Havaadis* हवादिस** Disasters

***Havaala* हवाला** Reference

***Havaas* हवास** Senses

***Hayaat* हयात** Life/Existence/Soul/Spirit

***Hayaat-o-mamaat* हयात-ओ-ममात** Life and death

***Hiile* हीले** Excuses

***Hijaz* हिजज़** Holy land for Islam/western province of S rabia which includes Mecca, Medina,

***Hijje* हिज्जे** Spelling/Division of words into phonetic syllables

***Hijrat* हिजरत** Migration

***Hikaarat* हिक़ारत** Contempt/Scorn/Disdain/Disgrace/Affront

***Hikaayat* हिक़ायत** Story/Tale/Narrative

***Hilaal* हिलाल** Crescent/New Moon

***Himmat-e-aalii* हिम्मत-ए-आली** High level of courage

***Himaayat* हिमायत** Support/Protection/Defence

***Hirmaan* हिरमां** Despondence/Disappointment/Misfortune/Denial (of a thing, to a person)

***Hissar-bandi* हिसार-बंदी** To fortify

***Hissar-e-zaat* हिसार-ए-ज़ात** Boundary of self

***Hosh-ruba* होश-रुबा** One who steals reason/Beloved

***Huduud* हुदूद** Limits/Boundaries

***Hungaam* हंगाम** A suitable moment/period of time

***Huruuf* हुरूफ़** Words

***Husuul* हुसूल** Acquisition/Attainment/Getting/Profit/Advantage

***Husn-e-amal* हुस्न-ए-अमल** Elegance of action/deliverance

***Husn-e-bayaan* हुस्न-ए-बयां** Elegant description

***Husn-parastii* हुस्न-परस्ती** Worship of beauty

***Huu* हू** Dread

Huuk **हूक़** Howl/Cry of pain/Shooting pain/ Extreme sorrow causing a deep sigh

Huvaidaa **हुवैदा** Manifest/ Clear/Evident/Open

Huzuur **हुज़ूर** Presence

I

Chaman tum se ibaarat hai bahaaren tum se zinda hain
Tumhaare saamne phuulon se murjhaayaa nahiin jaataa
Makhmoor Dehlvi

Muddat se iltifaat mire haal par nahiin
Kuchh to kajii hai dil men ki siidhii nazar nahiin
Imdad Ali Bahr

Tum takalluf ko bhii ikhlaas samajhte ho 'faraaz'
Dost hotaa nahiin har haath milaane vaalaa
Ahmad Faraz

Laakhon men intikhaab ke qaabil banaa diyaa
Jis dil ko tum ne dekh liyaa dil banaa diyaa
Jigar Moradabadi

Har ik ko nahiin hotaa irfaan mohabbat kaa
Har ik ko mohabbat kii jaagiir nahiin miltii
Anjana Sandhir

I

Ibaadat **इबादत** Prayer

Ibaarat **इबारत** Composition/Mode of expression/Passage of a book/Sentence/Word/Phrase/Style of writing

Ibrat **इब्रत**To take lesson/Warning/Admonition/An example

Ibrat-saraa-e-dahr **इब्रत-सरा-ए-डहर** World as an admonitory inn of warning

Idraak **इद्राक़** Senses

Iflaas **इफ़्लास** Poverty

Ifshaa **इफ़्शा** Disclosure

Iftaar **इफ़्तार** Breaking a fast/A slight repast with which a fast is broken

Iifaa **ईफ़ा** Fulfilment/Observance/Performance/Satisfaction

Iijaad **ईजाद** Invention/Contrivance

Iimaanii **ईमानी** Conviction and belief/Related to belief/Believer

IIsaar **ईसार** Sacrifice/Selflessness

Iltifaat **इल्तिफ़ात** Considerations/Cogitation/Contemplation/Reflection/Scrutiny/Examination

Iltimaas **इल्तिमास** Request

Iizaa **ईज़ा** Pain/Harm

Ijaabat **इजाबत** Acceptance/Answering or acceptance of prayer/ Compliance/Consent

Ijaara **इजारा** Monopoly/ Lease

Ijz **इज्ज़** Helplessness/ Powerlessness/ Humility/Modesty

Ik-guuna **इक-गूना** Continuous

Ikhlaas **इख़्लास** Sincerity/ Great affection

Ikhraaj **इख़राज** To remove or secretive

Ikhtilaaf **इख़्तिलाफ़** Dissension/ Disagreement/Discord/ Contradiction

Ikhtilaat **इख़्तिलात** Union

Ikhtitaam **इख़्तिताम** End/Completion/ Termination/Finish/ Close/Accomplishment

Ikhtiyar **इख़्तियार** Authority

Ikraam **इकराम** Honour/ Respect

Iksiir **इक्सीर** Cure-all medicine/Panacea/ Elixir/Effective medicine or advice

Ilhaam **इल्हाम** Divine inspiration/Revelation

Illaa **इल्ला** If not/ Otherwise/Besides

Iltifaat **इल्तिफ़ात** Love and affection

Iltijaa **इल्तिजा** Prayer/ Request/Supplication/ Petition/Entreaty

Iltizaam **इल्तिज़ाम** Being necessary or expedient

Imdaad **इम्दाद** Help/ Support/Assistance

Imkaan **इम्कां** Possibility

Imtiyaaz **इम्तियाज़** Discernment/ Distinction/ Prominence/Sense/ Judgement/Preference/ Discrimination

Inaayat **इनायत** Kindness/ Favours

Inab **इनब** Grapes

***Infiaal* इंफ़ियाल** Embarrassment/ Contrition/Penitence/ Shame

***Inkisaarii* इंकिसारी** Humbleness/Modesty

***Inquilaabaat-e-dahar* इन्क़िलाबात-ए-दहर** Changes/revolutions/ /vicissitudes of the world

***Intihaaen* इन्तिहाएं** Extremes

***Intikhaab* इंतिख़ाब** Selection/Election

***Intiqaal* इंतिक़ाल** Death/ Migration/Transfer

***Intiqaam* इन्तिक़ाम** Revenge

***Intisaab* इन्तिसाब** Lineage/ Descent/Relationship/ Connection/Dedication (of a book, etc)

***Intishaar* इंतिशार** Dispersion/Confusion/ Anxiety/Spreading abroad

***Iqbaal* इक़बाल** Good fortune/Admission/ Confession/Prosperity

***Iqraar* इक़रार** Promise/ Consent/Pledge

***Iram* इरम** Paradise

***Irfaan* इरफ़ान** Wisdom/ Enlightenment

***Irfanii* इर्फ़ानी** Enlightening/ Enlightened

***Irshaad* इर्शाद** Command/ Guidance

***Irtibaat-e-salaasil* इर्तिबात-ए-सलासिल** Connection of chains

***Isbaat* इस्बात** Affirmation/ Confirmation/ Verification/ Recognition/ Establishing

***Ishaaraton* इशारतों** Gesticulation/Hint/ Allusion/Indication/ Mark/Pointing to

***Ishrat* इश्रत** Pleasure/ Delight/Enjoyment/ Happiness

***Ishtiyaaq* इश्तियाक** Longing

Ism **इस्म** Denomination/Appellation/Noun/Name of a person, place or thing/Repeated recitation of any name of Allah/Sin

Ismat **इस्मत** Modesty/Maidenhood

Ismatein **इस्मतें** Modesty (pl)

Istiaara **इस्तिआरा** Metaphor/Simile

Istifaada **इस्तिफ़ादा** To gain advantage/Profit/Gain

Istiqbaal **इस्तिक़बाल** Reception/Welcoming a visitor

Istikhara **इस्तिख़ारा** Seek the good/Asking Allah to help make the choice between two

Istikhwan **इस्तिख़्वान** Bone

Isyaan **इस्यां** Sin

Itaab **इताब** Anger/Reproach/Reprimand/Rebuke

Itaab-e-muluuk **इताब-ए-मुलुक** Anger of the rulers

Ittihaad **इत्तिहाद** Union/Alliance/Concord

Izaarband **इज़ारबंद** Waist band

Izn **इज़्न** Permission

Izn-e-khiraam **इज़्न-ए-ख़िराम** Permission to promenade

Iztiraab **इज़्तिराब** Restlessness

Izzat-e-Saadat **इज़्ज़त-ए-सआदत** Respectable

J

Yaarab hazaar saal salaamat rahen huzuur
Ho roz jashn-e-iid yahaan jaavedaan basant
Muneer Shikohabadi

Do chaar baras jitne bhii hain jabr hii sah len
Is umr men ab ham se bagaavat nahiin hotii
Akram Mahmud

Ghaas men jazb hue honge zamiin ke aansuu
Paanv rakhtaa huun to halkii sii namii lagtii hai
Saleem Ahmed

Baad muddat ye jilaa kis ke hunar ne bakhshii
Baad muddat mire aaiine men chehre aae
Bakul Dev

Lachak hai shaakhon men jumbish havaa se phuulon men
Bahaar jhuul rahii hai khushii ke phuulon men
Ameer Minai

***Jaa* जा** Space/Place/Occasion

***Jaa-bajaa* जा-बजा** Here and there/Everywhere

***Jaabar* जाबर** Tyrant

***Jaada* जादा** Manner/Custom/Mode/Road/Route

***Jaahil* जाहिल** Illiterate/Uncouth/Ignorant

***Jaama-e-ehraam* जामा-ए-एहराम** Pious garb of pilgrim on pilgrimage to Mecca

***Jaam-e-tahuur* जाम-ए-तहूर** Allusion to nectar in heaven/Sacred drink of paradise

***Jaan-bar* जान-बर** A saviour/Being safe

***Jaan-e-nisaar* जान-ए-निसार** Devoted

***Jaan-fazaa* जान-फ़ज़ा** Life-invigorating

***Jaan-gusil* जान-गुसिल** Heart-breaking/Deadly/Life killer/Tormentor of life

***Jaanib* जानिब** Direction/Towards/In the direction of/Party or person as a side in a dispute or agreement

***Jaan-navaaz* जान-नवाज़** Offering life

***Jaan-nisaar* जान-निसार** Devoted/Fervent

***Jaan-sitaan* जान-सितां** Tyrant on life/Beloved

***Jaruub* जरूब** Sweeper/Broom

***Jaaruub-kash* जरूब-कश** Scavenger/Sweeper/Janitor

***Jaavedaan* जावेदां** Eternal/Everlasting/Perpetual

***Jabr* जब्र** Force

***Jafaa* जफ़ा** Oppression/injustice/Infidelity

***Jahl* जह्ल** Ignorance

***Jalaal* जलाल** Grandeur/Majesty/Splendour/Glory/Intensity/Velocity/Acceleration/Intensity

***Jallad* जल्लाद** Executioner

***Jalva-gar* जलवा-गर** Present/Manifest

***Jalaali* जलाली** One with ferocious anger

***Jamaal-e-kam-numaa* जमाल-ए-कम-नुमा** Less revealing beauty

***Jamaali* जमाली** Beautiful

***Jamhuuriyat* जम्हूरियत** Democracy

***Jamhuuriyat-navaaz* जम्हूरियत-नवाज़** Democrat/Rewarding democracy

***Jaraasiim* जरासीम** Bacteria

***Jaras* जरस** Bell rung to signal the departure of a caravan/Sweet voice/Humming sound/Bell on camel's neck

***Jasaaras* जसारस** Boldness/Courage

***Jast* जस्त** Leap/Bounce/Jump

***Jasta-jasta* जस्ता-जस्ता** Eclectically/Selectively/From here and there

***Jaulaan-gaah* जौलान-गाह** Arena

***Javaahir-khaana* जवाहिर-खाना** Jewel House

***Javaaz* जवाज़** Lawfulness/Permit/Permission

***Jazaa* जज़ा** Reward

***Jazb* जज़्ब** Absorption/Allurement/Magnetism/Attraction/Assimilation

***Jazba* जज़्बा** Spirit/Emotion/Passion/Feeling

***Jazb-e-dil* जज़्ब-ए-दिल** Absorption of heart

***Jazb-e-mohabbat* जज़्ब-ए-मोहब्बत** Absorption in love

***Jazbon* जज़्बों** Spirits

***Jaziira* जज़ीरा** Island

***Jhadiyaan* झड़ियाँ** Constant rain/Drizzle

***Jigar-chaak* जिगर-चाक** Torn heart

***Jigar-kharaash* जिगर-खराश** Heart-rending

***Jihat* जिहत** Direction/Side/Facet/Reason/Account/Direct

***Jilaa* जिला** Shining

***Jism-e-uryaan* जिस्म-ए-उरियाँ** Nude body

***Joban* जोबन** Bloom/Youth

***Johd* जोहद** Struggle

***Judaagaana* जुदागाना** Separate

***Jumbish* जुम्बिश** Motion/Agitation/Vibration/Jerk

***Juu* जू** Rivulet/Canal/Stream/Source of spring/Seeking/Seeker

***Juun* जूं** As/Which

***Juuebaar* जूएबार** Ravine/Source of rivulet or spring/Please where there are many ravines and canals

***Juz* जुज़** Part/Portion/Ingredient/(In binding) Signature/Folded form(of book)/Part of a book with 8/16 pp

***Juzv* जुज़्व** Besides/Except/Other than/Part

K

Chaahiye khud pe yaqiin-e-kaamil
Hausla kis kaa badhaataa hai koii
Shakeel Badayuni

Rihaa kar de kafas kii qaid se ghaayal parinde ko
Kisii ke dard ko is dil men kitne saal paalegaa
Aitbar Sajid

Kaisii kashish hai ishq ke tuute mazaar men
Mela lagaa huaa hai hamaare dayaar men
Jitendra Mohan Sinha Rahbar

Judaaiyon kii khalish us ne bhii na zaahir kii
Chhupaae apne gam-o-iztiraab maine bhii
Aitbar Sajid

Ranj se khuugar huaa insaan to mit jaataa hai ranj
Mushkilen mujh par padiin itnii ki aasaan ho gaiin
Mirza Ghalib

K

***Kaakh* काख़** Palace/Castle

***Kaamil* क़ामिल** Full/Entire/Complete/Perfect/Mature/Expert/Thorough/Accomplished

***Kaargah-e-dahar* कारगाह-ए-दहर** Factory of the world

***Kaasa* कासा** Goblet/Begging bowl

***Kaashaane* काशाने** House

***Kaatib* क़ातिब** Writer

***Kaavish* काविश** Effort/Endeavour/Search/

***Kaazib* क़ाज़िब** Liar/Mendacious/False/Fake

***Kabk-e-darii* क़ब्क-ए-दरी** Species of partridge found in the hills

***Kaf* कफ़** Palm

***Kafas* क़फ़स** Prison

***Kaf-e-dast-nigaaraan* कफ़-ए-दस्त-निगारां** Palm of hand painted

***Kafiil* कफ़ील** A security/Bail/Pledge

***Kaif* कैफ़** Pleasure/Ecstasy

***Kaifiyat* कैफ़ियत** Rapture/Ecstasy/Enjoyment/Condition/Circumstances/Narrative/Situation/Quality

***Kaj* कज** Awry/Crooked

***Kajii* कजी**Crookedness/Perversity/Raw

***Kalaam* क़लाम** Word/Speech/Conversation/Talk

***Kaliid* क़लीद** Key

***Kaliim* क़लीम** Speaker

***Kaliimii* क़लीमी** Quality of conversing with God/ Vision or sight of God

***Kaliisa* कलीसा** Church

***Kalma* कलमा** Muslim confession of faith/ Word/Saying/Part of speech

***Kamaal* कमाल** Perfection/ Completion/Complete/ Culmination/Limit/ Height

***Kamiin-gah* कमीं-गह** A lurking pace for ambush

***Kam-nigahii* कम-निगाही** Dim-sighted/ Short-sighted/ Miserliness/ Acrimony/Ignorance

***Kam-sin* कम-सिन** Young/ Tender/Beautiful

***Kam-zarf* कम-ज़र्फ़** Mean/ Vile/Silly

***Kamzor-tar* कमज़ोर-तर** Weaker

***Kaniiz* कनीज़** Slave-girl/ Maid servant/Female devotee

***Karam-farmaa* करम-फ़र्मा** Kind person

***Karb* कर्ब** Anguish/ Affliction/Agony

***Karda* कर्दा** Executed/ Effected/Made/Done

***Kariim* क़रीम** Bountiful/ Gracious/Merciful/ Epithet of God

***Kashaakash* कशाकश** Dilemma/Brawl/ Squabble/Struggle/ Grief and pain/ Stretching and straining

***Kashaan* कशां** Walking leisurely/Dragging/ Drawing/Attracting/ Bearing/Carried

***Kashish* कशिश** Attraction/ Allurement/Pull/ Drawing power

***Kashkol* कश्कोल** Bowl

***Kaund* कौंद** Dazzle/ Dazzling light/ Brightness

***Kaundan* कौंदन** Dazzling flash of light

***Kaun-o-makaan* कौन-ओ-मकान** World/Creation/Universe

***Kausar* कौसर** Lake or river in paradise/Heavenly spring

***Kenchulii* केंचुली** Skin of snake which is sloughed off

***Khadang* खडंग** Dimple

***Khaak* ख़ाक** Dust

***Khaak-aagushta-ba-khuun* ख़ाक-आगुश्ता-ब-ख़ून** Dust mixed woth blood

***Khaakistar* ख़ाकिस्तर** Ashes/Cinder

***Khaak-nashinon* ख़ाक-नशीनों** Ascetics

***Khaaksaaron* ख़ाकसारों** Low/Poor/Humble

***Khaal-o-aariz* खाल-ओ-आरिज़** Mole and cheek

***Khaala* ख़ाला** Vacuum/Space/Hollow

***Khaam* खाम** Raw/Unripe/Green/Crude

***Khaama* ख़ामा** Pen

***Khaana-barbaad* ख़ाना-बर्बाद** Ruined house

***Khaanqaah* ख़ानक़ाह** Monastery

***Khaanumma* खानुम्मा** Family/House/Home/Household goods

***Khaanamaan-barbaad* ख़ानमान-बर्बाद** Ruined/Miserable/Desolated/Unfortunate

***Khaanumaan-kharaab* ख़ानुमा-ख़राब** Wretched/Broken/Vanquished-hearted/Ruined

***Khaar* ख़ार** Thorn

***Khaashaak* ख़ाशाक** Dry grass

***Khaatam* खातम** Last/Ring/Seal/Stamp with inscription

***Khadang* खडंग** Small arrow/Tip of arrow/Poplar from which arrows are made

***Khadang-e-jasta* खडंग-ए-जस्ता** Arrow in flight

***Khadbadaae* खड़बड़ाए** Boiled/Simmered/Bubbled

***Khafaqaan* ख़फ़ाक़ान** Asphyxiation/Oppression/Supression

***Khafii* ख़ाफ़ी** Imperceptible

***Khaftaan* ख़फ़्तान** Dress worn over tunic/Ves worn under armour/Caftan

***Khair* ख़ैर** Goodness/Safety

***Khair-o-shar* ख़ैर-ओ-शर** Good and bad

***Khair-khvaahon* ख़ैर-ख़्वाहों** Well-wishers

***Khairaat* ख़ैरात** Charity

***Khajiil* ख़जील** Embarrass/Abashed/Ashamed/Penitent/Shame/Shyness/Bashfulness

***Khal* ख़ल** Skin

***Khalaa* ख़ला** Vacuum

***Khalaahon* ख़लाओं** Spaces

***Khaliil* ख़लील** Friend

***Khalish* ख़लिश** Misgiving/Unease/Anxiety/Worry/Prick

***Khalq* ख़ल्क़** Creation

***Khalvat* ख़ल्वट** Isolation/Seclusion/Solitude/Privacy/Private/Retirement/Retiring room or cell

***Khamiida* ख़मीदा** Bent

***Khanvatii* ख़नवती** Hermit/Recluse

***Khanda-zan* खंडा-ज़न** Setting up a laugh/One who sets up a laugh

***Khas* ख़स** Weak/Helpless

***Khasaraa* ख़सरा** Loss/Damage

***Khas-o-khaashaak* ख़स-ओ-ख़शाक** Straw and dried leaves

***Khashaak* ख़शाक** Dry eaves/Trash/Rubbish

***Khastagii* ख़स्तगी** Weariness/Exhaustion/Fatigue/Wounded state/Infirmity

Khat-o-khaal **ख़ट-ओ-ख़ाल** Features/Shape/Physique

Khavaas **ख़वास** Elite/Special/Peculiarities/Specialists/Favourite courtiers and attendants

Khayaabaan **ख़याबां** Flower bed

Khaaksaari **ख़ाक़सारी** Humility/Modesty

Khez **ख़ेज़** Evoking/Giving rise to

Khilat **ख़िलअत** Robe of honour

Khiraaj **ख़िराज** Paying tribute/obeisance

Khiraam **ख़िराम** Graceful walk

Khirad **ख़िरद** Wisdom/Reason

Khirad-mandii **ख़िरद-मंदी** Rationality

Khisht **ख़िश्त** Bricks

Khitaab **ख़िताब** Title/Address/Conversation/Speech

Khizaab **ख़िज़ाब** Dyeing/Tingeing hair and nails/Dye/Tincture

Khizar **ख़िज़र** Immortal

Khizr **ख़िज़्र** Prophet/Guide

Khosha-chiin **ख़ोशा-चीन** Recipient of benefaction

Khosha-e-gandum **ख़ोशा-गंदूम** Sheaf of wheat

Khubaan **ख़ुभां** Beauties/Sweethearts/Excellence/Virtue

Khud-aaraa **ख़ुद-आरा** Self-adorer/Arrogant

Khudaagahii **ख़ुदागही** Self-awareness

Khudaaiyaan **ख़ुदाइयां** Claims of being God

Khud-biin **ख़ुद-बीं** Self-conceited/Proud/Vain

Khuddaam **ख़ुद्दाम** Servants

Khud-raftagii **ख़ुद-रफ़्तगी** Drunkenness/Intoxication/Senseless/Madness

Khud-sar **ख़ुद-सर** Stubborn/Arrogant

Khufta **ख़ुफ्ता** Hidden

Khuld **ख़ुल्द** Paradise

Khuluus **ख़ुलूस** Sincerity/Integrity/Purity

Khur **ख़ुर** Cloven hoof/Act of eating

Khurd **ख़ुर्द** Young

Khurd-saal **ख़ुर्द -साल** Underage

Khurshiid **ख़ुर्शीद** Sun

Khuruus **ख़ुरूस** Domestic cock/The person who has more desire for lust/Sensualist

Khushaamad **ख़ुशामद** Flattery

Khush-aasaar **ख़ुश-आसार** Good Signs

Khush-fahm **ख़ुश-फ़हम** Optimist/Fanciful/One who looks at the bright side

Khush-fahmi **ख़ुश-फ़हमी** Good imagination

Khush-imkaanii **ख़ुश-इम्कानी** Optimism

Khushk **ख़ुश्क** Dry

Khush-khiraam **ख़ुश-ख़िराम** Good gait/Good walk

Khuu **ख़ू** Habit/Custom/Disposition/Behaviour

Khuubaan **ख़ूबां** Beauties/Fair ones/Sweethearts/Goodness/Virtue

Khuugar **ख़ूगर** Accustomed/Habituated

Khuun-bar **ख़ून-बार** Oozing blood/Shedding tears of blood

Khuun-chakaan **ख़ून-चकां** Blood oozing out/Dripping blood/Bleeding/Blood-drenched

Khuun-khvaar **ख़ून-ख़्वार** A beast of prey/Blood thirsty/Beastly

Khuun-rez **ख़ून -रेज़** Bloody/Cut throat/Murder

Khvaab-e-giraan **ख़्वाब-ए-गिरां** Deep/sound sleep/Unconscious/Indifference

Khvaabiidaa **ख़्वाबीदा** Sleepy/Drowsy

Khvaah **ख़्वाह** Wishing/Desiring/Soliciting/Willing/Requiring/Wanting

Khvaahaan **ख़्वाहां** Desirous/Candidate

Khvaan **ख़्वां** Reciter/Reader

Khvaar **ख़्वार** Shame/Dishonour/Disgrace/Abject/Wretched/Miserable/Distressed/Worried/Confounded

Khyaal-e-pukhta **ख़्याल-ए-पुख़्ता** Firm belief/Thought

Kibr **किब्र** Pride/Grandeur

Kiimiyaagar **कीमियाग़र** Alchemist

Kiina **कीना** Malice/Rancour/Grudge/Enmity

Kiina-saaz **कीना-साज़** Mean

Kinaaya **किनाया** Allusion/Innuendo

Kingra **किंगरा** Parapet/Pinnacle/Turret/Crest

Kirchen **किरचें** Shards/Pieces

Kirdaar **क़िरदार** Character/Deed/Conduct/Manner

Kisht **क़िश्त** Instalment/Sown field

Kishvar **किश्वर** Empire/Territories

Koh **कोह** Mountain

Koh-e-qaaf **कोह-ए-क़ाफ़** Caucasian Mountains/A lonely or inaccessible place/Abode of giants and fairies

Kohkan **कोहकन** Mountain digger

Kotaahii **कोताही** Deficency/Want/Brevity/Narrowness

Kuduurat **कुदूरत** Enmity/Resentment/Meenness/Ill-will

Kul **कुल** Whole/All/Entire/Aggregate/Each and every thing/ Complete/Family/ Tribe/ Lineage/Pedigree

Kulaah **कुलाह** Hat/Cap/Headgear/Bonnet

***Kulliyaat* कुल्लियात** Complete works

***Kuhan* कुहन** Ancient

***Kuhan-saal* कुहन-साल** Aged

***Kuhna* कुहना** Ancient

***Kun-fayaakuun* कुन-फयाक़ून** 'To be' or 'to exist' and 'it is'

***Kunj* कुंज** Secluded or solitary place/Confined space/Corner/

***Kushaa* कुशा** Airiness/Openness

***Kushaada* कुशादा** Wide/Ample/Open/Spacious/Uncovered/Expanded/Free/Frank/Loose

***Kushta* कुश्ता** Martyr/Residue after calcification/One desperately in love/Killed/Slain

***Kushtagaan* कुश्तागां** The one's desperately in love/ the slain/Those who have been killed

***Kushton* कुश्तों** Those killed

***Kuu-ba-kuu* कू-ब-कू** Everywhere

***Kuulhaa* कूल्हा** Hip/Buttock

***Kuuza-gar* कूज़ा-गर** Potter

L

Tuk dekh len chaman ko chalo laala-zaar tak
Kyaa jaane phir jien na jien ham bahaar tak
Meer Hasan

Dil vo hai ki fariyaad se labrez hai har vaqt
Ham vo hain ki kuchh munh se nikalne nahiin dete
Akbar Allahabadi

Lahad men kyuun na jaauun munh chhupaae
Bharii mahfil se uthvaayaa gayaa huun
Shad Azimabadi

Lauh-e-jahaan pe is tarah likkhaa gayaa huun men
Jis kaa koii javaab nahiin vo savaal huun
Khaleel Tanveer

Jhuut bhii sach kii tarah bolnaa aataa hai use
Koii luknat bhii kahiin par nahiin aane detaa
Zafar Sahbai

***Laag* लाग़** Spite

***Laagarii* लाग़री** Leanness/ Deficiency of virility/ Weakness

***Laal-o-gohar* लाल-ओ-ग़ौहर** Rubies and pearls

***Laala* लाला** Tulip

***Laala-o-gul* लाला-ओ-गुल** Tulips and flowers/ Beauty/Freshness/ Greenery/Pretty/ Beloved

***Laala-azaar* लाला-आज़ार** Tulip (Red) cheeked

***Laala-zaar* लाला-ज़ार** Bed of roses

***Laam* लाम** Greed/Avarice

***Laa-mahduud* ला-महदूद** Unlimited/Unbounded

***Laa-makaan* ला-मक़ान** Deity/Without place or abode

***Laa-ubaalii* ला-उबाली** Careless/Reckless/ Devil-may-care/ Insolent

***Laazim-o-malzuum* लाज़िम-ओ-मल्ज़ूम** Connected with one another

***Lab-e-gor* लब-ए-ग़ोर** On the verge of death/Near death

***Lab-e-goyaa* लब-ए-ग़ोया** Speaking lips

***Lab-e-juu* लब-ए-जू** Shore of a river

***Labrez* लबरेज़** Overflowing/Brimful

***Lagaavat* लगावट** Attachment/Adherence/ Intimate connection/ Intimacy/Closeness/ Liason/Sexual intercourse

***Lagan* लगन** Pans

***Lagzish* लग़्ज़िश** Blunder/ Error/Shake/ Tremble

***Lahad* लहद** Cavity where dead body is kept in a grave

***Lahza* लहज़ा** A moment/A minute/A glance/Wink of an eye

***Lahza-ba-lahza* लहज़ा-ब-लहज़ा** Moment by moment

***Lail-o-nahaar* लैल-ओ-नहार** Night and day/ Times/Circumstances

***Lailatul-qadr* लैलतुल-क़द्र** Night of power (27th night of Ramadan when the Q'ran began to be revealed to the Prophet of Islam

***Lakht* लख़्त** Piece/ Bit/Portion/Part/ Little/Continuously/ Immediately

***Laqab* लक़ब** Appellation of honour/Title/Epithet/ Name in which qualities of a person are known

***Larzish* लर्ज़िश** Quivering/ Shivering

***Lashkar* लश्कर** Army/ Encampment

***Lauh* लौह** Tablet/Plank/ Board on which one writes

***Lek* लेक** But/Still/Yet/ Nevertheless

***Lobaan* लोबां** Frankincense/Resin burnt for its smell

***Luknat* लुक़नट** Stammer/ Stammering/Stuttering

***Lutma* लुटमा** Injured

M

Zindagii shama kii maanind jalaataa huun 'nadiim'
Bujh to jaauungaa magar subah to kar jaauungaa
Ahmad Nadeem Qasmi

Sarak kar aa gaiin zulfen jo in makhmuur aankhon tak
Main ye samjhaa ki mai-khaane pe badlii chhaaii jaatii hai
Nushur Wahidi

Ham se shaayad motabar thahrii sabaa
Jis ne ye gesuu sanvaare aap ke
Ibn-E-Mufti

Havaa to hai hii mukhaalif mujhe daraataa hai kyaa
Havaa se puuchh ke koii diye jalaataa hai kyaa
Khurshid Talab

Muntazir huun main kafan baandh ke sar se 'aajiz'
Saamne se koii khanjar nahiin aayaa ab tak
Ajiz Matvi

***Maaal* मआल** End/Result/Consequence/Place of refuge/Place of return

***Maaash* मआश** Subsistence/Livelihood

***Maaaz* मआज़** Shelter/Refuge/At the mercy of/In the protection of

***Maadar-e-dahr* मादर-ए-दहर** Mother of world or time/Eternity

***Maaduum* मअदूम** Extinct/Non-existent/Absent/Annihilated/Wanting/Not found/Not existing

***Maail* माइल** Inclined/Bent/Attracted

***Maajraa* माजरा** State/Condition/Incident/Happening

***Maamuure* मामूरे** Thriving

***Maandagii* मांदगी** Tiredness/Fatigue/Indisposition/Illness

***Maane* माने** Hindrance/Bar/Impedimet/Barrier/Preventing/Forbidding/Obstructing

***Maanii-khez* मायनीखेज़** Evoking meaning

***Maaniind* मानींद** Just as/Like/Resembling

***Maanuus* मानूस** Associated/Familiar/Attached/Friendly/Intimate/Used to/Well-known

***Maarkaa* मार्का** Victory/Place or scene of battle/Battle-ground/Fight/Strife

***Maarke* मार्के** Battles/ Expeditions/ Adventures/ Contests

***Maashii* माशी** Black

***Maa-siva* मा-सिवा** Besides/ Moreover/Over and above/Apart from/ Other than/ Except

***Maaya-e-naaz* माया-ए-नाज़** Wealth that is a cause of pride

***Maaaz-allah* मआज़-अल्लाह** I seek the protection of God/ Heaven defend me/At the mercy of God/God forbid

***Maazarat* मअज़रत** Excuse/Apology/Plea

***Maazii* माज़ी** Past

***Maazi-e-marhuum* माज़ी-ए-मरहूम** Dead past

***Maazuul* मअज़ूल** Suspended

***Maaaz* मआज़** In the protection of/At the mercy of

***Maazuur* मअज़ूर** Helpless/ Disabled

***Mabaadaa* मबादा** God forbid/Lest/Let it not be/Never

***Madaar* मदार** Axis/Pivot/ Basis/Centre

***Madfan* मद्फ़न** Tomb/ Grave

***Madfuun* मद्फ़ूं**Interred/ Buried/Concealed/ Hidden/Underground (as treasure)

***Madfuun-e-dariya* मद्फ़ूं-ए-दरिया** Water-burial

***Magas* मगस** Honey-bee

***Maghfirat* मग़फिरत** Remission/Forgiveness/ Absolution/Deliverance/ Salvation/Pardon

***Magmuum* मग़मूम** Sad/ Afflicted/Grieved/ Sorrowful

***Magrib* मग़रिब** West/ Sunset/Sundown/ Evening/Sunset prayer/ Europe and Western countries

Magruur **मग़रूर** Proud

Magz **मग्ज़** Brain/Cerebra/Kernel/Chief substance or essence of anything/Intellect

Mah **मह** Moon

Mahaar **महार** Bridle/Rein

Mahbas **महबस** Prison/Confinement

Mahbuus **महबूस** Prisoner/Captive/Confined/Frenzied/Detained/Arrested/Jailed/Incarcerated

Mahduud **महदूद** Limited/Restricted

Mah-e-siyaam **मह-ए-सियाम** Moon of Ramzan

Mahi **महि** Fish

Mahjuur **महजूर** Lovelorn/Foresaken/Rejected/Cut-off/Separated/Forbidden/Prohibited/Prevented

Mahmil **महमिल** Camel's litter/Saddle of camel

Mahkuum **महकूम** Slave/Servant/Subject/The ruled/Subjugated/Under control

Mahr **महर** Sun

Mahram **महरम** Confidant

Mahruum **महरूम** Deprived

Mahshar **महशर** Judgement day, doomsday

Mahshar-e-khayaal **महशर-ए-ख़्याल** Pandemonium of thoughts/Bedlam

Mahsuul **महसूल** Tax/Custom/Octroi/Excise

Mahv **मह्व** Absorbed/Fascinated

Mahaviiyyatein **महवीय्यतें** Absorption/Being totally lost in thought

Mah-e-daagii **मह-ए-दाग़ी** Bemished moon

Mahruum **महरूम** Deprived of/Debarred/Excluded/Refused

Mahtaab **महताब** Moon

Mah-vash **मह-वश** Moon-faced

Mahzuun **महज़ून** Melancholy/Melancholic

Mai-kash **मय-कश** Drinkers

Majaaz **मजाज़** Competent/Lawful/Authorised/Legally authorised

Majma **मजमा** Collection

Majrooh **मजरूह** Wounded/Bruised

Makaan **मकां** Space/House

Makhmuur **मख़्मूर** Intoxicated

Makharab **मख़रब** Spoiler

Makiin **मकीं** Dweller/Resident/Inhabitant/Inmate/Settler

Makr **मक्र** Deceit/Cheating

Maktab **मक़तब** School

Maktuub **मक़तूब** Letter/Epistle/Written/Message/Writing

Malaamat **मलामत** Reproach/Rebuke/Reprehension/Censure/Blame

Malak **मलक** Angel/Divine messenger

Malbuus **मलबूस** Clothes/Clothed/Garments

Maluul **मलूल** Sad/Dejected/Melancholy/Weary

Mamaat **ममात** Death

Mamnuun **मम्नूं** Obliged/Thankful/Grateful/Beholden

Maane-e-parvaaz **माने-ए-परवाज़** Hindrance to flight

Mansoor **मंसूर** Victorious

Mansuub **मंसूब** Appointed/Nominated/Fixed/Related to manifestation

Manzar **मंज़र** Sight/View

Maqaam **मक़ाम** Place/Position/Occasion/Dwelling

Maqduur **मक़दूर** Means/Resources/Power/Ability/Authority

Maqmuur **मक़मूर** Sad

Maqsood **मक़्सूद** Intended/Proposed

Maqtaa **मक़्ता** Last couplet of a ghazal which often contains the *takhallus* (pen-name)

Maqtal **मक़्तल** Place of slaughter

Maraahil **मराहिल** Stages

Maraasim **मरासिम** Relationships/Customs/Rules

Marg **मर्ग़** Death

Marhabaa **मरहबा** Greeting/Welcome/Hail/Bravo

Marhale **मरहले** Stage

Markab **मरक़ब** Anything in which one is carried

Marmar **मर्मर** Marble

Martaba **मर्तबा** Degree/Office/Rank/Status/Turn/Time/Class

Masaafat **मसाफ़त** Journey/Distance

Masaaib **मसाइब** Plural of musiibat/Calamities/Misfortunes/Miseries/Discourse on the sufferings of the Karbala martyrs

Masaail **मसाइल** Problems/Questions/Propositions/Precepts

Masal **मसल** Like/For example/Proverbial/Adage/Saying/Maxim

Masarrat **मसर्रत** Happiness

Masduud **मस्दूद** Closed/Shut/Obstructed/Stopped

Mashaqqat **मशक़्क़त** Labour/Pain/Toil/Trouble

Mashiyyat **मशिय्यत** Pleasure/Will/Wish/God's will

Mashq **मश्क़** Exercise/Practice/Drill

Masiihaa-nafas **मसीहा-नफ़स** One who's breath is as effective as the breath of Christ/Expert doctor

Masjuud **मस्जूद** Adored/God/To whom one bows or worships

Maskh **मस्ख़** Distorted/Deformed/Misshapen/Mutilation

***Maskon* मस्कों** Sycophancy/Butter

***Maslahat* मस्लहत** Prudent measure/Policy/Good thing

***Maslahatan* मस्लहतन** Hidden reason

***Masruur* मस्रूर** Glad/Cheerful/Delighted

***Mass-e-havaa* मस्स-ए-हवा** Touch of breeze

***Mastuur* मस्तूर** Concealed/Hidden/Covered/Veiled/Written/Expressed

***Mataa* मताअ** Capital/Commodity/Assets/Property/Possessions/Goods/Valuables/Merchandise

***Matlaa* मतला** Opening rhyming couplet of a ghazal/East/Place of rising sun. Both lines contain the *qaafiya* (trailing rhyme) and *radiif* (words repeated after the rhyme)

***Matlab* मत्लब** Meaning/Motive/Aim

***Matluub* मतलूब** Desired/Longed for/That which is sought/Demanded

***Matn* मत्न** Text

***Mauhuumii* मौहूमी** Imagined/Fancied/Supposed

***Maujzan* मौजज़न** Tumultous/Stormy/Exciting

***Mauquuf* मौक़ूफ़** Dependent on/Depend upon/Suspended/Potponed/Delayed/Deferred/Stopped/Abolished

***Mauzuu* मौज़ू** Subject/Topic/Object

***Mayaar* मयार** Quality

***Mayyat* मय्यत** Corpse/A dead body

***Mazaa-daar* मज़ा-दार** Enertaining

***Mazaahib* मज़ाहिब** Religions

***Mazaamiin* मज़ामीन** Essays/Articles

***Mazaazii* मज़ाज़ी** Figurative/Metaphorical

Mazhar **मज़हर** Manifestation/ Phenomenon

Mazkuur **मज़्कूर** Expressed/Mentioned/ Recorded/Related/ Mention

Mazluum **मज़्लूम** Injured/ Oppressed/Wronged/ One who is wronged

Mazmuun **मज़मून** Essay/ Article/Subject/ Objective/Topic/ Purport/Sense/Context

Mehraab **मिहराब** Pricipal niche in the mosque from where the imam conducts prayers/ Arched niche

Mehr-e-darakhshaan **मैहर-ए-दरख़्शां** Bright sun

Mehrii **मैहरी** Head-stall/ That part of a bridle that encompasses the head

Mehr-o-mah **मैहर-ओ-माह** Sun and moon

Mehr-o-vafaa **मैहर-ओ-वफ़ा** Love and fidelity

Mehvar **मैहवर** Axis/Center

Memaar **मेमार** Mason/ Architect/Builder/ Inventor/Founder/ Leader

Meraaj **मेराज** Ladder/ Ascension

Meyaar **मेयार** Standard measure or weight/ Touchstone/Yardstick

Miim **मीम** Shape

Miiraas **मीरास** Estate/a bequest/Ancestral/ Property

Miirzaaii **मीरज़ाई** Princedom/Gentility/ Pride/Nobles/Prices/ Children of Mughals

Miisaaq **मीज़ाख़** Covenant/ Treaty

Miizaan **मीज़ां** Scale

Milk-o-maal **मिल्क-ओ-माल** Country/Wealth

Millat **मिल्लत** Community

Mimbar **मिंबर** Pulpit

Minnat-kash **मिन्नत-कश** Desirous/Obliged

Minnat-kash-e-davaa **मिन्नत-कश-ए-दवा** Obliged to medicine

Minnat-kash-e-sahra **मिन्नत-कश-ए-सहरा** Desirous of desert

Mirg **मिर्ग़** Death

Mishal **मिशल** Light/ Beacon

Misii **मिसी** Lip colouring substance

Miskin **मिस्किन** Understate/Less speech

Misl-e-habaab **मिस्ल-ए-हबाब** Resembling a bubble

Mistar **मिस्तर** Pages with ruled lines/Foot rule

Mizgaan **मिज़ग़ां** Eye lashes

Moajaza **मोअजज़ा** Miracle

Moajize **मोअजीज़े** Wonders/Miracles

Moattar **मोअत्तर** Perfumed/ Fragrant

Mohkam **मोहकम** Firm/ Strong/Stable/Fortified

Mohtasib **मोहतसिब** Supervisor of observance of law and punishment

Mominaan-e-saadiq **मोमिनां-ए-सादिक़** True believer

Mongiyaa **मोंगिया** Of the colour of red coral

Motabar **मोतबर** Reliable/ Trustworthy

Motadil **मोतदिल** Moderate

Motaqid **मोतक़िद** Adherent/Believer in faith, creed or person/ Faithful servant/Friend

Muamme **मुअम्मे** Puzzles

Muayyan **मुअय्यं** Fixed/ Established/Definite

Mubaashir **मुबाशिर** One who lies with a woman for sex/One who commences or undertakes an affair

Mubaddal **मुबद्दल** Altered/ Changed/Exchanged/ Substituted

***Mubham* मुबहम** Ambiguous/Equivocal/ Dubious/Doubtful/ Hidden/Indistinct

***Mubtala* मुब्तला** Engaged/ Afflicted/Entangled/ Involved/Busy

***Mudaam* मुदाम** Eternal/ Perpetual/Everlasting/ Permanently/ Eternally

***Mudaaraat* मुदारात** Courtesy/Politeness/ Hospitality

***Mudaava* मुदावा** Cure

***Mufiid* मुफ़ीद** Beneficial/ Useful/Profitable/ Advantageous

***Muflis* मुफ़्लिस** Poor

***Mugaan* मुगां** Tavern-keeper/Spiritual guide

***Mugbacha* मुगबचा** Boy serving wine in a tavern

***Mugiilaan* मुगीलां** Babool/ Acacia

***Mugtanim* मुगतनिम** Opportune/ Advantageous/ Worthwhile

***Muhiit* मुहीत** Encircling/ Surrounding/ Circumambient

***Mujrimaana* मुजरिमाना** Criminal/Cuplable

***Mukhaalif* मुख़ालिफ़** Opposite/Enemy/ Unfavourable/An opponent

***Mukhaalifat* मुख़ालिफ़त** Contravention/ Breach/Conflict/ Dispute/Infringement/ Obstruction/ Opposition

***Mukhtaari* मुख़्तारी** Independence/Power/ Authority

***Mukhtalif* मुख़्तलिफ़** Different

***Mukhtsar* मुख़्तसर** Brief

***Mulhid* मुल्हिद** Atheist/ Unbeliever/Heretic/ Pagan/Infidel

Mulk-e-baqaa **मुल्क-ए-बक़ा** The afterlife

Muluuk **मुलूक** Ruler

Munaajaat **मुनाजात** Prayer/Invocation/ Hymn/Supplication to God/Whispering/Secret conversation

Munawwar **मुनव्वर** Illuminated/Lustrous/ Radiant

Mundril **मुन्द्रिल** Ear-ring/ Stud

Munhadim **मुन्हदिम** Demolished

Munhasir **मुन्हसिर** Dependent on/Resting on/Besieged

Munim **मुनिम** Benefactor/ Donor/Grantor

Munkir **मुंकिर** Non-believer

Munsif **मुंसिफ़** Judge/ Arbitrator/Just/Equitable

Muntashir **मुंतशिर** Wide-spread/Dispersed/ Diffused/Propagated/ Divulged/Distracted/ Bewildered

Muntazir **मुन्तज़िर** One who waits/Expectant

Muqaabil **मुक़ाबिल** In front(of)/In comparison(with)/ Face-to-face/Opposite/ Converse/Confronting

Muqaam **मुक़ाम** Dwellin/ Place/Position/ Occasion

Muqaddam **मुक़द्दम** Above all/Antecedent/Chief/ Prior

Muqaddas **मुक़द्दस** Holy/ Sanctified/Consecrated

Muqaffal **मुक़फ़्फ़ल** Lock/ Locked

Muqarrar **मुक़र्रर** Pre-determined/ Established/Fixed/ Repeating/Recurring/ Repeatedly/Encore/ Once more

Muqiim **मुक़ीम** Inhabitant/ Residing/Fixed/ Stationed

Muraasalaat **मुरासलात** Correspondence

Muraqqa **मुरक़्क़ा** Album/Portfolio

Murassaa **मुरस्सा** Written in rhyming and grandiose words/Studded with jewels & precious stones

Murassa-saaz **मुरस्सा-साज़** Jeweller/Inlayer

Muravvat **मुरव्वत** Kind-heartedness/Affection/Humanity

Murdaar **मुर्दार** Squalid/Impure/Ugly/Corpse/Carrion

Murda-shuu **मुर्दा-शू** Washer of dead bodies

Murgaan **मुर्गां** Birds

Murgh **मुर्ग़** Cock/Bird

Muriid **मुरीद** Disciple

Musaahib **मुसाहिब** Friend/Comrade/Associate/Companion

Musalla **मुसल्ला** Prayer mat

Musalsal **मुसलसल** Constant

Musavvir **मुसव्विर** Painter/Sculptor/Photographer

Musavvarii **मुसव्वारी** Painting/Photography

Mushahida **मुशाहिदा** Witnessing/Contemplation

Mushavvash **मुशव्वश** Disturbed/Perplexed/Embroiled/Intricate

Mushtaaq **मुश्ताक़** Longing for/Desirous/Eager/Yearning/Longing

Mushtahar **मुश्तहर** Advertised/Announced/Proclaimed

Mushtail **मुश्तैल** Excited/Inflamed/Kindled/Blazing

Mushtamil **मुश्तमिल** Containing/Comprising/Including/Inclusive (of)

Mushtaqbil **मुश्तक़बिल** Future/Future tense

Mushtarak **मुश्तरक** Common/Joint

Musht-e-ustukhvaan **मुश्त-ए-उस्तख्वां** Mere skeleton/Very weak body

***Mustaaar* मुस्तार**
Borrowed/Obtained or taken as a loan

***Mustafa* मुस्तफ़ा** Chosen/Select/A title for Prophet Muhammad

***Mustanad* मुस्तनद**
Authentic/Reliable/Confirmed/Authoritative/Certified/Incontrovertible

***Mustaqil* मुस्तक़िल**
Persistent/Assiduous/Consistent/Fixed/Permanent/Firm/Stable/Constant/Enduring/Durable

***Mutaala* मुताला** Study

***Mutaalba* मुताल्बा** Asking for/Demand/Claim/Requirements/Due

***Mutlaq* मुत्लक़** Wholly/Altogether/Universal/Absolute

***Mutlaqan* मुत्लक़न**
Absolutely/Entirely

***Mutmain* मुत्मैन** Satisfied

***Mutrib* मुतरिब** Singer

***Muttafiq* मुत्तफ़िक़**
Agreeing/Consenting/United

***Muu-e-dost* मू-ए-दोस्त**
Beloved's hair

***Muvaafaqat* मुवाफ़क़त**
Accord/Agreement/Concord/Conformity/Consonance/Affinity/Correspondence

***Muzhda* मुज़दा** Good news/Good tidings

***Muzmahil* मुज़्महिल**
Infirm/Weak/Fatigued/Exhausted/Sad/Anguished/Stressed

***Muzmar* मुज़्मर** Concealed/Latent/Hidden

***Muztar* मुज़्तर** Distressed/Afflicted/Anxious/Troubled

***Muztarib* मुज़्तरिब**
Afflicted/Agitated/Uneasy/Confused/Restless

N

Ham khud bhii hue naadim jab harf-e-duaa niklaa
Samjhe the jise patthar vo shakhs khudaa niklaa
Hilal Fareed

Gam o nashaat kii har rahguzar men tanhaa huun
Mujhe khabar hai main apne safar men tanhaa huun
Makhmoor Saeedi

Chalo lahuu bhii charaagon kii nazr kar denge
Ye shart hai ki vo phir raushnii ziyaada karen
Manzoor Hashmi

Goggle lagaa ke aankh par chalne lage hasiin
Vo lutf ab kahaan nigah-e-niim-baaz kaa
Hashim Azimabadi

Har qadam duuri-e-manzil hai numaayaan mujh se
Merii raftaar se bhaage hai bayaabaan mujh se
Mirza Ghalib

N

Naachaar **नाचार** Helpless

Naadim **नादिम** Repentant/Ashamed/Contrite/Apologetic

Naaf **नाफ़** Navel

Naa-gahan **ना-गहन** Unexpected/Accidental

Naa-haq **ना-हक़** Uncalled for

Naa-karda **ना-करदा** Not done

Naa-khush-andeshii **ना-ख़ुश-अंदेशी** Lack of ideas/Lack of advises

Naama **नामा** Letter/Book/History/Treaty

Naama-bar **नामा-बर** Messenger

Naama-o-paighaam **नामा-ओ-पैग़ाम** Exchange of letters or messages/Correspondence/Letter and message

Naa-muraadii **ना-मुरादी** Disappointment/Failure/Misfortune

Naamvar **नामवर** Renowned/Celebrity/Well-known/Celebrated

Naa-padiid **ना-पदीद** Concealed/Invisible/Hidden

Naaqa **नाक़ा** She-camel

Naaquus **नाक़ूस** Conch shell

Naar **नार** Fire

Naara **नारा** Exclamation

Naa-rasaaiyon **ना-रसाइयों** Not accessible

***Naarasaaon* नारसाओं** Beyond reach/ Unreachable

***Naara-zanii* नारा-ज़नी** Slogan shouting

***Naarii* नारी** Full of fire/ Fiery/Hellish

***Naashaad* नाशाद** Cheerless/ Joyless/Sadness/Sorrpw/ Despondency/Woe/ Gloom

***Naa-shuniidan* ना-शुनीदां** Unheard

***Naa-tamaam* ना-तमाम** Unfinished/Deficient/ Incomplete/Imperfect

***Naavak* नावक** Arrow

***Naavak-e-naaz* नावक-ए-नाज़** Arrows of love

***Naazaan* नाज़ां** Proud/ Conceited/Arrogant

***Nadaamat* नदामत** Regret/Self-reproach/ Repentance/Shame

***Nadiim* नदीम** Friend/ Companion/Favourite courtier of the king/ Confidant

***Nafas* नफ़स** Breath/Soul/ Spirit/Self

***Nafas-e-baaz-pasiin* नफ़स-ए-बाज़-पसीन** Last gasp of breath

***Nafat* नफ़त** Profit

***Nafsiyaat* नफ़्सियत** Psychology

***Nagma-e-shaadii* नग़मा-ए-शादी** Song of happiness

***Nagmagii* नग़मग़ी** Lyricism

***Nahaar* नहार** Lunch

***Nahang* नहंग** Alone/ Solitary/Free from care/ Unconcerned/Naked/ Shameless

***Nahv* नह्व** Path/Mode/Way

***Nairang* नैरंग** Deceit/ Trick/Magic/Sorcery/ Miracle/Anything new or strange

***Najaat* नजात** Deliverance/ Escape/Salvation/ Liberation/Absolution

***Najd* नज्द** A horse found in Najd province of S Arabia/High ground in S Arabia

Nakhl **नख़्ल** Date tree/ Sapling/Tree

Nakhl-e-hirmaan **नख़्ल-ए-हिरमान** Tree of destiny

Nakhvat **नख़वत** Pride/ Conceit/Haughtiness

Naksh **नक़्श** Print/Mark/ Impression/Engraving/ Charm

Namruud **नमरूद** A powerful God/One who cast Abraham into the fire/Cruel/Arrogant/ Haughty

Nang-e-vajuud **नंग-ए-वजूद** Shame on existence

Naqqaaraa **नक़्क़ारा** Big drums/Voice/Wish

Naqd-o-nisyah **नक़द-ओ-निसयाह** Cash & credit/ Pleasure of the world now vs borrowing the happiness which will be found in the hereafter

Naqs **नक़्स** Flaw/Blemish/ Diminution

Naqsh **नक़्श** Ikon/Picture

Naqsh-e-kuhan **नक़्श- ए -कुहन** Old belief/ custom/building/ Ancient imprint

Naqsh-o-nigaar **नक़्श-ओ-निगार** Embellishment

Nashaat **नशात** Joy/ Cheerfulness

Nasheb **नशेब** Slope/ Descent

Nasheman **नशेमन** Nest

Nashtar **नश्तर** Lancet/ Cutter

Nashv-o-numaa **नश्व-ओ-नुमा** Growth/Increase

Nasiim **नसीम** Light breeze

Natwaan **नतवां** Impotent

Nau-khez **नौ-ख़ेज़** Youthful/Young/Newly sprung up/Adolescent

Nauha **नौहा** Plaintiveness/ Lamentation/Requiem/ Dirge

Nauha-e-gam **नौहा-ए-ग़म** Dirge of sorrow

Nauhagar **नौहागर** Mourner/Elegy singer/ Wailing

***Nauha-garii* नौहा-ग़री** Mourning/Lamenting

***Nauha-khvaani* नौहा-ख़्वानी** Lamenting/weeping

***Nau-rusta* नौ-रस्ता** Fresh/New blooming

***Navaa* नवा** Expression

***Navaa-garii* नवा -ग़री** Singing/Chanting

***Navaa-saaz* नवा-साज़** Musical instrument player

***Navaa-sanj* नवा-संज** Song

***Navaa-sanjii* नवा-संजी** Singing/Chanting

***Navaaz* नवाज़** Cherishing/Soothing/Caressing/Playing on music/Performer

***Navaazish* नवाज़िश** Favour/Politeness/Patronage

***Navardii* नवर्दी** Wandering

***Navishte* नविश्ते** Letters/Documents

***Nayaab* नयाब** Rare

***Nazar-shanaas* नज़र-शनास** Knowing/Clever

***Naziir* नज़ीर** Example/Instance/Like

***Nazm-e-gulistaan* नज़्म-ए-गुलिस्तां** Order/Arrangement of the garden

***Nazr* नज़्र** Offering/Gift/Present/Bribe

***Nazzaargii* नज़्ज़ार्गी** Spectacle

***Neamat* नेअमत** Gift

***Neze* नेज़े** Spears/Reeds from which pen is made

***Nezon* नेज़ों** Spears/Lances

***Nifaaq* निफ़ाक़** Discord/Enmity

***Nigaar* निग़ार** Figure/Effigy/Portrait/Picture/Beloved/Idol

***Nigaaraan* निगारां** Painted

***Nigahbaan* निगहबान** Guard

***Niguun* निगूँ** Hanging down/Turned upside down/Inverted/Bent

Niguun-bakhton **निगूँ-बख़्तों** Those with declining fortunes

Nihaan **निहां** Hidden

Niim-baaz **नीम-बाज़** Half-closed/Intoxicated

Niim-khvaabii **नीम-ख़्वाबी** Drowsiness/Half-asleep/Dozing/Lethargy

Nisaa **निसा** Women/Ladies/The female sex

Nisaab **निसाब** Syllabus/Curriculum

Nisaar **निसार** Sacrifice

Nisbat **निज़्बत** Relation/Affinity

Nisbat-e-ishquii **निज़्बत-ए-इश्क़ी** Relationship of love

Nishast **निशस्त** Session/Seat

Nisyaan **निस्यां** Forgetfulness/Amnesia/Oblivion

Niyaaz **नियाज़** Offering/Need/Desire/Petition/Supplication

Niyyaz-bandii **नियाज़-बंदी** Humbleness/Obedience/Humility/Entreaty

Niyyat-e-shauq **निय्यत-ए-शौक़** Intention to love

Nizaam **निज़ाम** System/Rule/Regulation/Practice/Order/Arrangement

Nujuum **नुजूम** Stats

Nukta-daan **नुक़्ता-दान** Discerning/Subtle/Sagacious/Of penetrating intellect

Nukta-saraa **नुक़्ता -सरा** Connoisseur of fine nuances/Appreciator

Nukta-varo **नुक़्ता-वरों** Those who understand nuances

Numaayaan **नुमायां** Apparent/Prominent/Visible/Conspicuous

Numuud **नुमूद** Show/Display/Appearance/Manifestation

***Numuudaar* नुमूदार** Apparent/Conspicuous/Visible

***Numuud-e-suvar* नुमूद-ए-सुवर** Growth of great patience

***Nuqta* नुक़्ता** Dot

***Nuqta-e-sabz* नुक़्ता-ए-सब्ज़** Green dot

***Nur-afshaan* नूर-अफ्शां** Light diffused

***Nutq* नुत्क़** Power of speech and reasoning

***Nuurii* नूरी** Full of light

P

Jab main ne kahaa dil miraa paamaal kiyaa kyuun
Kis naaz se bole ki mohabbat kii sazaa thii
Muztar Khairabadi

Thodaa saa aks chaand ke paikar men daal de
Tuu aa ke jaan raat ke manzar men daal de
Kaif Bhopali

Nafrat bhii usii se hai parastish bhii usii kii
Is dil saa koii ham ne to kaafar nahiin dekhaa
Alamtaab Tishna

Kii tark-e-mai to maail-e-pindaar ho gayaa
Mainn tauba kar ke aur gunahgaar ho gayaa
Dagh Dehlvi

Har aadmii men the do chaar aadmii pinhaan
Kisii ko dhuundne niklaa koii milaa mujh ko
Fuzail Jafri

P

***Paa-ba-giil* पा-ब-गील**
Restrained/Immobile/Helpless/Prisoner

***Paa-basta* पा-बस्ता** Stable/Firm/Established/Strong/Arrested/Feet bound

***Paaedaar* पा-ए-दार**
Permanent/Durable/Steady/Firm

***Paaedaarii* पा-ए-दारी**
Durability

***Paa-e-kham* पा-ए-ख़म**
Bottom of the glass

***Paaemaal* पा-ए-माल**
Ruined/Devastated/Subdued

***Paa-e-nigaah* पा-ए-निगाह**
At a glance

***Paaentii* पाएनती** Foot of tomb or grave or bedstead/Towards head

***Paakbaaz* पाकबाज़**
Chaste/Pure/Honest/Virtuous/Austere/One who abstains from sin

***Paimaaii* पैमाई**
Measurement

***Paamaal* पामाल** Trodden/Trampled/Ruined

***Paan-khurda* पान-ख़ुर्दा**
Chewing of betel leaf

***Paara-e-dil* पारा-ए-दिल**
Piece of heart

***Paarsaa* पार्सा** Pure/Chaste/Abstemious/Holy/Virtuous person

***Paarsaaii* पारसाई** Purity/Chastity

***Paas* पास** Regard

***Paasang* पासंग**
Counterweight/Balance

Paasbaan **पासबां** Guard/Sentinel/Watchman

Passbaan-e-aql **पासबां-ए-अक़्ल** Guard of intuition

Paash **पाश** Breaking

Paash-paash **पाश-पाश** Broken

Paayaab **पायाब** Shallow/Fordable (can be forded)/Within one's depth/Ford

Paighaam-e-hayaat-e-javedaan **पैग़ाम-ए-हयात-ए-जावेदां** Message of eternal love

Paiham **पैहम** Together/Continuous/Successively/Close

Paimaaii **पैमाई** Measurement/Measure

Paimaan **पैमान** Vow/Promise

Paikar **पैकर** Form/Appearance/Visage/Figure/Body

Paikaar **पैकार** War/Battle/Contest

Paikaan **पैकान** Tip of arrow

Paik-e-tasavvur **पैक-ए-तसव्वुर** Arrow of fancy/Reach of experience

Paiharan **पैहरन** Dress/Apparel

Pairaae **पैराए** Ways/Methods/Masnners/Styles/Conduct

Paivasta **पैवस्ता** Contiguous/Joined/Linked/United/Old/Clinging close/Sticking close

Par-afshaanii **पर-अफ़शानी** Act of flapping the wing

Parastish **परस्तिश** Worship/Adoration

Parda-daar **पर्दा-दार** Privy

Parda-darii **पर्दा-दारी** Removing the veil/Revealing the truth/Fault-finding/Ignominy/infamy

Par-e-sarhad **पस-ए-सरहद** Beyond boundaries

Parizaad **परिज़ाद** Born of a fairy/Beautiful

Parkaar **परकार** Compass

Partav **पर्तव** Reflection/Shadow/Image/Light/Ray

Partav-e-khur **पर्तव-ए-ख़ूर** Sun's reflection

Pas **पस** Behind/After

Pas-e-marg **पस-ए-मर्ग़** After death

Pas-e-mohabbat **पस-ए-मोहब्बत** Regard for love

Pashemaan **पशेमां** Embarrassed/Penitent/Repentent/Ashamed

Pashemaanii **पशेमानी** Embarrassment

Paziiraaii **पज़ीराई** Acceptance/Reception/Entertainment/Welcome/The act of accepting

Pechdaar **पेचदार** Complex/Complicated

Pech-o-kham **पेच-ओ-ख़म** Perplexity/Difficulty

Peer-e-mugaan **पीर-ए-मुगां** Keeper of tavern

Pesh-e-yaar **पेश-ए-यार** In front of lover

Pesh-khema **पेश-ख़ेमा** Prelude/Harbinger

Pesh-tar **पेश-तर** Before/Formerly/Prior to

Phaag **फाग़** Red colour thrown on each other on Holi

Piir **पीर** Holy man/Spiritual guide/Cunning and shrewd man/Founder of a religious order/Old man

Pindaar **पिंडार** Pride/Conceit

Pinhaan **पिन्हां** Concealed/Hidden

Pistaan **पिस्तां** Breast

Posh **पोश** Hide

Poshiida **पोशीदा** Conceled/Hiffen/Secret/Covered/Veiled/Secretly/Covertly/Hunter's trap

Pur-asraar **पुर-असरार** Mysterious

Pursish **पुर्सिश** Interrogation/Enquiry/Asking/Questioning/Visiting the sick

***Pur-soz* पुर-सोज़** Burning/ Lighted/Blazing

***Pusht-panaahii* पुश्त-पनाही** Support/ Backing/Background

***Putliyaan* पुतलियां** Pupils/ Puppets

Q

Qaasid payaam-e-shauq ko denaa bahut na tuul
Kahnaa faqat ye un se ki aankhen taras gaiin
Jaleel Manikpuri

Mire vajuud ke andar hai ik qadiim makaan
Jahaan se main ye udaasii udhaar letii huun
Asima Tahir

qalaq aur dil men sivaa ho gayaa
dilaasaa tumhaaraa balaa ho gayaa
Altaf Hussain Hali

Ye ijz hai ki qanaaat hai kuchh nahiin khultaa
Bahut dinon se vo khair-o-khabar se baahar hai
Abul Hasanat Haqqi

Duurii huii to us ke qariin aur ham hue
Ye kaise faasle the jo badhne se kam hue
Unknown

Q

***Qadir* क़ादिर** Powerful/Almighty

***Qaafiyaa* क़ाफ़िया** The rhyming pattern. The *radif* is preceded by words or phrase with the same end rhyme pattern called the *qaafiyaa*

***Qaafiya-paimaaii* क़ाफ़िया-पैमाई** Measuring rhyme

***Qaail* क़ाइल** Agree/Consent/Convince/Acknowledgement

***Qaalib* क़ालिब** Mould/Frame/Body

***Qaamat* क़ामत** Height/Stature

***Qaasid* क़ासिद** Messenger

***Qadah* क़दह** Goblet

***Qadah-khvaar* क़दह-ख़्वार** Wine drinker

***Qadam-bosii* क़दम-बोसी** Kissing the feet/Homage/Obeisance

Qadgan क़दग़न Injunction/Prohibition

***Qadiim* क़दीम** Old/Ancient/Traditional

***Qahba* क़हबा** Adulteress/Whore/Prostitute

***Qahr* क़हर** Anger/Rage/Wrath/Fury/Calamity/Curse/Violence/Oppression/Conquering

***Qaht* क़हत** Dearth

***Qalandarii* क़लंदरी** Ascetic/Mystical/Going against the established social or religious norms

***Qalaq* क़लक़** Regret/Discomfort/Trouble/Anxiety/Deep regret/Sorrow

***Qalb* क़ल्ब** Heart/Main body of the army

***Qalbii* क़ल्बी** Relating to the heart/Heartfelt/Fake/Counterfeit

***Qamar* क़मर** Moon

***Qaleel* क़लील** Poor/Scarce/Bare/Meagre

***Qanaaat* क़नाअत** Contentment

***Qandeel* क़ंदील** Lamp/Lantern/Candlestick

***Qariin* क़रीं** Closely resembling/Fellow/Member of a society/Close/Near/Connected/Friend

***Qariine* क़रीने** Decorations

***Qariin-e-jaan* क़रीन-ए-जां** Close to life

***Qasaas* क़सास** Retort

***Qasas* क़सस** Retribution/Vengeance

***Qash-ariiraa* कश-अरीरा** Horror making hair stand erect/Trembling with fear

***Qashqa* क़श्क़ा** Mark on forehead/*Tika*

***Qasr* क़स्र** Palace

***Qata* क़ता** To finish

***Qat-e-taalluq* क़त-ए-तआल्लुक़** Break in relations

***Qatl-gaah* क़त्ल-गाह** Place of slaughter/Abattoir

***Qattaala* क़त्ताला** Slayer/Killer

***Qattaalii* क़त्ताली** Killing/Slaying/Related to murder

***Qaul* क़ौल** Promise/Adage/Word/Speech/Quotation

***Qaul-o-qaraar* क़ौल-ओ-क़रार** Promise and acceptance/Treaty/Mutual agreement

***Qaus* क़ौस** Arch/The area of a circle/Bowl

***Qavaa* क़वा** Body parts

***Qayaam* क़याम** Stay

***Qazaa* क़ज़ा** Fate/Death/ Omitted prayer or fast/ Lapse

***Qaziya* क़ाज़िया** Tiff/Court case/Judgement

***Qibla* क़िब्ला** Holy mosque at Mecca/Kaaba/ Direction to which Muslims bow during prayer

***Qibla-numaa* क़िब्ला-नुमा** Instrument to find direction of Mecca/ Compass/Facing west

***Qissa-khvaan* क़िस्सा-ख़्वां** Story-teller/Reciter of tales

***Qudsiya* क़ुद्सिया** Pure/ Holy

***Qufl* क़ुफ़्ल** Padlock

***Qufl-e-abjad* क़ुफ़्ल-ए-अब्जद** A lock with numbers/A kind of coded-lock/Puzzle

***Quwwat* क़ुव्वत** Strength

R

Go raahzan kaa vaar bhii kuchh kam na thaa magar
Jo vaar kaargar huaa vo rahnumaa kaa thaa
Akbar Hameedi

Kyuunkar badhaauun rabt na darbaan-e-yaar se
Aakhir koii to milne kii tadbiir chaahiye
Mardan Ali Khan Rana

Ajiib hii thaa mire daur-e-gumrahii kaa rafiiq
Bichhad gayaa to kabhii laut kar nahiin aayaa
Iftikhar Arif

Zaraa se rizq men barkat bhii kitnii hotii thii
Aur ik charaag se kitne charaag jalte the
Atiiqullah

Umr bhar khul nahiin paate hain rumuuz-o-asraar
Log kuchh saamne rah kar bhii nihaan hote hain
Quaiser Khalid

R

Raad **राड** Thunder

Raaegaan **राएगां** Useless/ In vain/Fruitless/ Wasted

Raaegaanii **रायगानी** Uselessness/ Fruitlessness

Raah-e-adam **राह-ए-अदम** Last journey/Death

Raah-numaa **राह-नुमा** Guide/Leader/Pilot/ Conductor

Raahzan **राहज़न** Highway robbers

Raal **राल** Salliva/Spittle

Raam **राम** Tame/Pacified/ Submissive

Raanaaii-e-khayaal **रानाई-ए-ख़्याल** Beauty or elegance or sublimity of ideas

Raas **रास** Be suitable

Raasaaii **रासाई** Access/ Approach/Entrance/ Arriving/Skill/ Acuteness/Sharpness of mind/Perspicacity/Reach

Raasha **रअशा** Tremor

Raba **रबा** Quarters

Rabt **रब्त** Conection/ Relation/Bond/Intimacy

Rabt-e-baahamii **रब्त-ए-बाहमी** Mutual attachment

Rabt-e-qalbii **रब्त-ए-क़ल्बी** Emotional bond/ Intimacy

Radiif **रदीफ़** Refrain word or phrase. Both lines of the *matlaa* and the second line of all shers must end with the same refrain

***Rafaaqaton* रफ़ाक़तों** Friendships/ Companionships

***Rafat* रफ़त** Highness/ Eminence

***Rafiiq* रफ़ीक़** Friend

***Rafta* रफ़्ता** Past

***Rafta-e-raftaar* रफ़्ता-ए-रफ़्तार** Speed of the bygone ages

***Rafta-rafta* रफ़्ता-रफ़्ता** Slowly/Gradually

***Raftagaan* रफ़्तग़ां** Those who are dead and gone/ Departed

***Ragbat* रग़बत** Curiosity/ Interest/Inclination

***Rag-e-jaan* रग-ए-जां** Jugular vein

***Rag-e-taak* रग-ए-ताक** Vines of grape

***Rahbar* रहबर** Guide

***Rahbaraan-e-qaum* रहबरां-ए-क़ौम** Leaders of the nation

***Rahiim* रहीम** Merciful

***Rahiin* रहीं** Mortgaged/ Indebted

***Rah-navard* राह-नवर्द** Vagrant/Wanderer

***Rah-ravaan* राह-रवां** Followers

***Rah-ravaan-e-khaak-basar* राह-रवां-ए-ख़ाक-बसर** Travellers living on dust

***Rah-rau* राह-रौ** Travel companion

***Rahzan* रहज़न** Highwayman/Robber

***Rakaab* रक़ाब** Stirrup

***Rakaat* रक़अत** Portion of Islamic prayer

***Rakhna-haa-e-siina* रख़ना-हा-ए-सीना** Obstacles of the heart

***Rakhsh* रख़्श** Brilliance/ Splendour/Rays or reflection of life/Horse/ Rustom's horse/White & red mixed colour

***Rakhsh-e-umr* रख़्श-ए-उम्र** Horse of life/Fast passing life

***Rakht-e-safar* रख़्त-ए-सफ़र** Things needed on a journey/Goods of travel

***Ramiida* रमीदा** Terrified

***Raqaabat* रक़ाबत** Rivalry (especially in love)

***Raqam* रक़म** Chronicle/ Put on record/Amount

***Raqsaan* रक़्सां** Dancing

***Rasaa* रसा** Reached/ Arriving/Capable/ Penetrating/Of keen understanding/Sharp

***Rasaaii* रसाई** Access/ Reach/Approach/ Entrance/Sharpness (of mind)/Perspicacity

***Rasan* रसन** Rope

***Rasan-o-daar* रसन-ओ-दार** Death by hanging

***Rashha-e-qalam* रशहा-ए-क़लम** Compositions of pen

***Rashk* रश्क़** Jealousy/ Envy/Malic/Spite

***Rashk-e-chaman* रश्क़-ए-चमन** Envy of the garden

***Rashk-e-mah* रश्क़-ए- मह** Envy of the moon/ Jealous of moon/Very beautiful

***Rasman* रस्मन** As a matter of tradition or custom/ Formally

***Rasm-o-raah* रस्म-ओ-राह** Traditions and ways

***Rau* रौ** Flow

***Raulaa* रौला** Riot/Brawl/ Furore/Uproar

***Rauunat* रऊनत** Pride/Awe

***Rauzaan* रौज़ान** Hole/ Window/Skylight

***Ravaa* रवा** Right/Lawful/ Admissible/Current

***Ravish* रविश** Pathway/ manners

***Razaa* रज़ा** State of being content/Pleasure/ Consent/Assent/ Approval/ Permission

***Reg* रेग़** Sand

***Reg-e-ravaan* रेग़-ए-रवां** Flying sands/Shifting sands

***Rehn* रेह्न** Mortgage/ Pledge/Bail/Security

***Reza* रेज़ा** Scrap/Piece/ Atom

***Rifaaqat* रिफ़ाक़त** Companionship/ Friendships

***Rifat* रिफ़त** Height

***Rikaab* रिक़ाब** Stirrup

***Rind-e-laa-ubaalii* रिन्द-ए-ला-उबाली** Careless drinker/The one who madly drinks

***Risaalon* रिसालों** Magazines

***Rivaak* रिवाक** Canopy/ Roof in front of a tent/ Gallery in front of the house/Curtain stretched before the door of a house or tent

***Rivaayat* रिवायत** Traditions

***Riyaa* रिया** Hypocrisy/ Pretence/Dissimulation

***Rizq* रिज़्क़** Daily bread/ Subsistence/Livelihood

***Rizvaan* रिज़वां** Paradise

***Roab* रोआब** Fear/Awe

***Roz-e-jazaa* रोज़-ए-जज़ा** Doomsday/Judgement day/Day od resurrection

***Roz-e-panj-shamba* रोज़-ए-पंज-शम्बा** Thursday

***Rujuua* रुजूअ** Recourse/ Appeal/Bias/Reference/ Turning (toward)/ Inclination/Bent/ Returning/ Leaning

***Rukh-e-nikuu* रुख़-ए-निकू** Beautiful face

***Rumuuz* रुमूज़** Secrets

***Ruqa* रुक़ा** Note/Letter

***Rusvaa* रुस्वा** Despondent/ Dishonoured

***Rutba* रुत्बा** Honour

***Ruu* रू** Basis/ Countenance/Face

***Ruubaahii* रूबाही** Cunning

***Ruu-ba-shaam* रू- ब-शाम** Face towards evening

***Ruuh-e-ravaan* रूह-ए-रवां** Moving spirit/Flowing soul/Life and soul (of party)

***Ruu-posh* रू-पोश** Hidden/ Gone into hiding/ Absconder/Wrapper/ Concealed

***Ruu-siyaah* रू-सियाह** Black-faced/Disgraced/ Ignominious/Sinner

***Ruudaad* रूदाद** Report/ Statement/Minutes/ Narrative/Story

S

Sadaaqat ho to dil siinon se khinchne lagte hain vaaiz
Haqiiqat khud ko manvaa letii hai maanii nahiin jaatii
Jigar Moradabadi

Ab to saraab hii se bujhaane lage hain pyaas
Lene lage hain kaam yaqiin kaa gumaan se ham
Rajesh Reddy

Burii sarisht na badlii jagah badalne se
Chaman men aa ke bhii kaantaa gulaab ho na sakaa
Arzoo Lakhnavi

Vo taaza-dam hain nae shoabde dikhaate hue
Avaam thakne lage taaliyaan bajaate hue
Azhar Inayati

Kah rahaa hai shor-e-dariyaa se samundar kaa sukuut
Jis kaa jitnaa zarf hai utnaa hii vo khaamosh hai
Natiq Lakhnavi

S

***Saaat* साअत** Time/Moment/Hour/Clock

***Saaatein* साअतें** Moments

***Saabiqa* साबिक़ा** Intimacy/Dealings

***Saabit* साबित** Established/Firm/Fixed/Stable/Prove/Confirm/Manifest/Constant/Stationary/

***Saadaat* सादात** Descendents of Md and Fatima/Respectful

***Saadat* सादत** Blissfulness

***Saada-lauh* सादा-लौह** Simpleton

***Saadir* सादिर** Flushed/Surprised/Anxious/Worried/Proceeding/Issued/Passed

***Saadmaanii* सादमानी** Happiness

***Saaebaan* साएबान** Canopy

***Saahib-e-kitaab* साहिब-ए-क़िताब** One to whom God reveals a book/Divinely ordained prophet/Author/Man of book

***Saahib-e-maqduur* साहिब-ए-मक़दूर** Person with ability

***Saail* साइल** Beggar/Applicant/Petitioner/Interrogater/Questioner

***Saakin* साक़िन** Resident/Stationary/Tranquil

***Saalahaa* सालहा** Years

***Saane-e-kudrat* साने-ए-क़ुदरत** Creator of nature/God

Saaneha **सानेहा** Accident/ Occurrence

Saang **सांग** Disguise/ Mimicry/Acting a part in a play

Saanii **सानी** Chaff and straw mixed with grain and water as fodder

Saaqii-e-kausar **साक़ी-ए-क़ौसर** Prophet Muhammad as the steward of the heavenly spring Kausar

Saarbaan **सारबां** Camel driver

Sabaa **सबा** East wind/ Buying wine to sell/ Historical city of Empress Bilkiis contemporary of Prophet Sulaimna

Sabaat **सबात** Permanence/ Constancy/Stability

Sabiih **सबीह** Comely/ Handsome

Sabiil **सबील** Strategy/ Resource

Sabt **सब्त** Inscription/ Inscribed

Sadaa **सदा** Sound/Call/ Ring/Bell/Shout

Sadaa-nafas **सदा-नफ़स** Breath of air

Sadaa-noshi **सदा-नोशी** Absorbing sound

Sadaaqat **सदाक़त** Truth/ Veracity/Fidelity/ Truthfulness/Verity/ Sincerity

Sadaf **सदफ़** Shell

Sadiq **सादिक़** Sincere

Sadqe **सदक़े** Alms/ Offerings

Saf **सफ़** Queue

Saf-ba-saf **सफ़-ब-सफ़** One by one

Saffaak **सफ़्फ़ाक़** Cruel/ Tyrant

Safiihon **सफ़ीहों** Stupid persons

Safiiraan **सफ़ीरां** Ambassadors

Sahaab **सहाब** Cloud

Sahaafii **सहाफ़ी** Journalist

Sahba **सहबा** Wine, especially red

***Sahal-angaarii* सहल-अंगारी** Carelessness/ Taking easy

***Sahal-talab* सहल-तलब** Easy-going

***Sahar-e-kaazib* सहर-ए-क़ाज़िब** Time just before daybreak/False dawn

***Sahar-gaahii* सहर-ग़ाही** Awakening

***Saharii* सहरी** Of or relating to the dawn/Of morning

***Sahiifa* सहीफ़ा** Leaf/ Page/Magazine/Book/ Volume/Periodical/ Book revealed to a divinely ordained prophet

***Sahn* सहन** Courtyard

***Sahraa* सहरा** Desert/ Wilderness/Plain

***Sahraa-gard* सहरा-ग़र्द** Desert wanderer

***Sahuulat* सहूलत** Ease/ Facility

***Sahv* सह्व** Error/Mistake/ Negligence

***Saii* सई** Effort/Endeavour/ Advance payment

***Sail* सैल** Flood

***Sail-e-ashk* सैल-ए-अश्क़** Flood of tears

***Saili* सैली** Slap

***Sakhii* सख़ी** Generous person/Donor

***Sakht-jaan* सख़्त-जां** Callous

***Sakht-jaanii* सख़्त-जानी** Hard life

***Salaa-e-aam* सला-ए-आम** Open invitation to all

***Salaasil* सलासिल** Chains/ Shackles

***Saliib* सलीब** Crucifix

***Samaaat* समाअत** Hearing power

***Samaaii* समाई** Capacity/ Capability/Patience

***Saman* समन** Jasmine

***Saman-khaanon* समन-ख़ानों** Idol houses/ Temples

***Samar* समर** Fruit

***Samarvar* समरवर** Laden with fruit

***Samo* समो** High/Tall/Elevated

***Sanaa-khvaan* सना-ख़्वां** Praise reciter/One who praises

***Sanad* सनद** Charter/Diploma/Patent

***Sang-e-giraan* संग-ए-गिरां** Heavy stone

***Sanobar* सनोबर** Pine tree

***Sapedii* सपेदी** Grey hair

***Sar* सर** On/At

***Saraab* सराब** Mirage

***Saraapaa* सरापा** Human figure from head to foot

***Sar-afraaz* सर-अफ़्राज़** Promoted/Exalted

***Sar-ba-sar* सर-ब-सर** Entirely/Whole

***Sar-ba-kaf* सर-ब-कफ़** One who is willing to die/Bravery

***Sar-chashma-e-baqaa* सर-चश्म-ए-बक़ा** Source of elixir of immortality

***Sardaadgaan* सरदादगां** Chiefs

***Sard-mehrii* सर्द-मैहरी** Indifference/Cold attitude/Negligence/Ingratitude

***Sarf* सर्फ़** Use/Busy/Expenditure/Extravaganza/Expense

***Sarfaraaz* सर्फ़राज़** Eminent/Exalted/Distinguished

***Sarf-e-tapish* सर्फ़-ए-तपिश** Use of heat

***Sargarm* सरगर्म** Busy/Active

***Sar-giraan* सर-गिरां** Restless/Anxious

***Sargoshii* सरग़ोशी** Whisper/Gossip/Speaking in a low voice

***Sariir-e-khaama* सरीर-ए-ख़ामा** Scratching sound made by the pen

***Sarisht* सरिश्त** Temperament

***Sar-kashii* सर-कशी** Rebellion

***Sarmastii* सरमस्ती** Intoxication

***Sar-naame* सर-नामे** Letter-heads

***Sar-niguun* सर-निगूं** Vanquished

***Sarosh* सरोश** Angel/ Heavenly voice/ Supreme intellect

***Sarpat* सर्पट** Gallop/Run with fast speed/Quickly

***Sarsabz* सरसब्ज़** Fertile/ Fruitful/Productive/ Prosperous/ Flourishing/Verdant

***Sarsarii* सरसरी** Cursorily/ Casually/Lacking in attention

***Sarshaarii* सरशारी** Intoxication

***Sarv* सर्व** Cypress

***Sarzad* सर्ज़द** To be committed/Occurred/ Happened

***Sataaish* सताइश** Accolade/ Praise/Appreciation/ Eulogy

***Sataaish-gar* सताइश-गर** One who praises/ appreciates

***Sauubaton* सौबतों** Difficulties

***Sauda* सौदा** Frenzy/ Madness/Goods/ Trade/Purchase

***Saudaa-garii* सौदा-ग़री** Melancholia/Trade

***Saudaaii* सौदाई** Lovesick/ Melancholic/Crazy/ Insane

***Savaab* सवाब** Reward/ Recompense/ Requital/Reward esp of obedience to God/ Meritorious act

***Savaabit* सवाबित** The fixed stars/Stars

***Sayyaare* सय्यारे** Planets

***Sayyargaan* सय्यारगां** Planets

***Sazaavaar* सज़ावार** Deserving of punishment

***Sazaa-yab* सज़ा-यब** Awarded with punishment/Penalized or sentenced person

***Seb-e-gabgab* सेब-ए-गबगब** Dimple in chin

***Sehn* सेहन** Courtyard

***Shaadaab* शादाब** Verdant/ Blooming green

***Shaadmaan* शादमां** Happy

***Shaahid* शाहिद** Eye witness

***Shaakii* शाक़ी** One who complains

***Shaam-e-gariibaan* शाम-ए-गरीबां** Evening full of calamities/Night of mourners/Mourning night observed by Shias in Muharram

***Shaan-e-kariimii* शान-ए-क़रीमी** Majesty of God's kindness

***Shaana* शाना** Adult/Elder/ Decent/Smart/Elegant/ Glory/Comb/Shoulder

***Shab-e-taar* शब्-ए-तार** Dark night

***Shab-gaziida* शब्-ग़ज़ीदा** Injured or hurt by night

***Shabiih* शबीह** Image/ Portrait/Picture/ Resemblance

***Shabistaan* शबिस्तां** Bed chamber/Covered part of a mosque

***Shab-rang* शब्-रंग** Dark coloured

***Shadeed* शदीद** Intense

***Shafaaf* शफ़ाफ़** Clear/ Limpid/Transparent/ Bright/Open to public scrutiny/Morally correct

***Shafaq* शफ़क़** Evening twilight

***Shagaf* शग़ाफ़** Inclination/ Interest/Liking/ Fondness/Enthusiasm

***Shagufta* शगुफ़्ता** Refreshed, blooming

***Shaguftagii* शगुफ़्तग़ी** Cheerfulness/Delihjt/ Pleasure

***Shaguufa* शगूफ़ा** Bud

***Shahaadat* शहादत** Witness/Evidence/ Testimony/Martyrdom

***Shahar-aaraa* शहर-आरा** Embellishing/ Decorating city

Shahbaaz **शाहबाज़** Brave man/Young man

Shah-e-mardaan **शाह-ए-मर्दां** King of heroes/ Hazrat Ali

Shaahid **शाहिद** Witness/ Bystander

Shahr-aaraa **शहर-आरा** Embellishing or decorating city

Shahr-e-badar **शहर-ए-बदर** Banish/Exile

Shahr-e-jaan **शहर-ए-जां** City of life/Self/Body

Shahr-e-khamoshaan **शहर-ए-खामोशां** Cemetry

Shah-nashiin **शाह-नशीं** Throne

Shahriyat **शहरियत** Citizenship

Shahvat **शैहवत** Lust/ Sensuality/Sexual urge

Shah-zor **शाह-ज़ोर** Powerful

Shaidaa **शइदा** Infatuation/ Enamored

Shajar **शजर** Tree

Shakal-e-shabaahat **शकल-ए-शहाबत** Visage and resemblance

Shakebaaii **शकेबाई** Patience/Tolerance/ Endurance

Shams **शम्स** Sun

Shanaas **शनास** Knowing/ Acquainted with/ Intelligence/ Knowledge

Shanaasaa **शनासा** Familiar

Shanaasaaii **शनासाई** Acquaintance/ Knowledge

Shanaasii **शनासी** Awareness/The act of knowing/The act of identifying

Shanaavar **शनावर** Swimmer

Sharaf **शरफ़** To be or become exalted

Sharar **शरर** Spark/Flash

Sharh **शर्ह** Interpretation/ Explanation

Sharhen **शर्हें** Explanations/ Interpretations

Sharmsaar **शर्मसार** Ashamed/Regretting

Sharraah **शर्राह** Interpreter

Shashdar **शश्दर** Perplexed/Astonished/ Confounded

Shauq **शौक़** Eagerness/ Fondness/Zeal/Ardour/ Desire/Hobby/Passion/ Longing/Pleasure

Shaayaan **शायां** Fit (for)/ Suitable/Desirable

Shefta **शेफ़्ता** Enamoured with love

Sheva **शेवा** Manner

Sheva-e-guftaar **शेवा-ए-गुफ़्तार** Style of speech

Shiaar **शिआर** Method/ Custom/Countersign

Shiaarii **शिआरी** Conditioned to

Shiddat **शिद्दत** Force/ Severity/Intensity

Shifaa **शिफ़ा** Healing/ Cure/Recovery

Shikam**शिकम** Stomach

Shikam-ser **शिकम-सेर** Full stomach

Shiir **शीर** Milk

Shiir-o-shakkar **शीर-ओ-शक्कर** Close intimacy/ Hand in glove/Very close and intimate

Shiiraaza **शीराज़ा** Binding (of book)/Arrangement

Shiisha-e-saaat **शीशा-ए-साअत** Hourglass

Shirk **शिर्क** Polytheism

Shirkat **शिर्कत** Participation/ Partnership/ Company

Shitaab **शिताब** Quick/ Speed/Haste

Shitaabii **शिताबी** Quickness/Haste/ Speed/Swiftness/ Uneasiness/Anxiety/ Perturbation

Shoala-zaar **शोअला-ज़ार** Field of embers/Light/ Flames

Shoabadagar **शोअबदागर** Illusionist

Shoabadakaaron **शोअबदाकारों** Jugglers

Shoabde **शोअब्दे** Magic/ Tricks

Shohra **शोहरा** Fame/ Reknown/Reputation/ Acknowledgement

Shohra-e-aafaaq **शोहरा-ए-आफ़ाक़** Of worldwide fame

Shoriidgii **शोरीदग़ी** Confusion/Tumult/ Rebellion/Craziness/ Passion

Shorish **शोरीश** Tumult

Shubh **शुब्ह** Doubt

Shuhra **शुहरा** Fame

Shuhuud **शुहूद** Anything that is apparent and can be seen/Friday/Day of resurrection

Shumaar **शुमार** Countig/ Numbering/Number/ Account

Shuniidan **शुनीदां** Listening

Shuruua **शुरूअ** Beginning

Shusta-mizaaj **शुस्ता-मिज़ाज** Cultivated temperament

Shuuur **शुऊर** Consciousness

Sifaal **सिफ़ाल** Earthenware/Earth/ Soil/Clay/Cover/Shell (esp decorated with flowery design)

Sifat **सिफ़त** Attribute/ Quality/Trait/ Characteristic/Fetire/ Epithet/Praise

Sifaat **सिफ़ात** Qualities

Siflaa **सिफ़्ला** Sordid/Vile/ Base/Ignoble/Low/ Mean

Siim **सीम** Silver

Siim-tan **सीम-तन** Silver-bodied/Fair

Siirat **सीरत** Quality/ Nature/Disposition/ Character

Sila **सिला** Reward

Sin **सिन** Age

Sinaan **सिनां** Spears

***Sipar* सिपर** Shield/Bold/Undaunted/Secure/Assistant

***Sitaan* सितां** Place where anything dwells

***Sitam-zariif* सितम-ज़रीफ़** One who practices tyranny in a subtle way

***Sitaara-e-saharii* सितारा-ए-सहरी** Morning star

***Sivaa* सिवा** But/Over and above/Except

***Siyaam* सियाम** Ramzan

***Siyah-faam* सियाह-फ़ाम** Dark comlexion

***Soam* सोअम** Conceit/Arrogance

***Sog* सोग** Grief/Lamentations

***Sogvar* सोगवर** Sad/Grieved

***Sohbatein* सोहबतें** Company

***Sokhta* सोख़्ता** Burnt/Grieved/Dejected/Lovesick/A piece of burning wood/Blotting paper/Slow match/Flint

***Soz* सोज़** Burning/Sorrow/Heart-burning

***Soz-e-taaza* सोज़-ए-ताज़ा** New passion

***Subh-dam* सुबह-दम** Early morning/Dawn

***Subh-e-azal* सुबह-ए-अज़ल** Beginning of eternity/Time when existence came to being

***Subh-e-kaazib* सुबह-ए-काज़िब** False morning/Time just before daybreak

***Subh-gaahii* सुबह-ग़ाही** Relating to dawn or morning

***Subha* सुबहा** Rosary

***Subuk-ruuh* सुबुक़-रूह** Cheerful/Merry/Jovial

***Subuu* सुबू** Goblet/Jar/Pitcher/Glass/Cup

***Sukhan* सुख़न** Talk/Speech/Dialogue/Converse/News/Discourse/Poetry

***Sukhan-e-sakht* सुख़न-ए-सख़्त** Harsh or difficult words

***Sukhan-varii* सुख़न-वरी** Eloquence/Poetry/The art of composing poetry

***Sukr* सुक्र** To be or become intoxicated/ Intoxicant or alcoholic drink/Intoxication/ Drunkenness

***Sukuut* सुकूत** Silence/ Quietness/Peace

***Sulh-e-kul* सुलह-ए-कुल** Perfect reconciliation/ Definitive treaty/Peace-loving/Peace with all

***Sumbul* सुम्बुल** Hyacinth

***Summa-aahaa* सुम्मा-आहा** Act of sighing in pain

***Surat-nigaararaan* सूरत-निगारां** Painters/ Artists

***Surkh* सुर्ख़** Red

***Sust-al-vajuud* सुस्त-अल-वजूद** Lazy bones

***Sutuun* सुतूं** Pillar

***Suu* सू** Directions

***Suud* सूद** Profit/Interest/ Gain

***Suurat-e-bayaan* सूरत-ए-बयां** Style/way of narrative

T

Khvaab dekhaa thaa mohabbat kaa mohabbat kii qasam
Phir isii khvaab kii taabiir men masruuf thaa main
Khalid Malik Sahil

Tadbiir mere ishq kii kyaa faaeda tabiib
Ab jaan hii ke saath ye aazaar jaaegaa
Meer Taqi Meer

Unhen to sitam kaa mazaa pad gayaa hai
Kahaan kaa tajaahul kahaan kaa tagaaful
Bekhud Dehlvi

Uljhaa hai magar zulf men taqriir kaa lachhaa
Suljhii huii ham ne na sunii baat tumhaarii
Muneer Shikohabadi

Yaad men khvaab men tasavvur men
Aa ki aane ke hain hazaar tariiq
Bayan Meeruthi

T

Taa-ba-kujaa **ता-बा-कुजा** Up to where, whither/ How far/How long/ Till when

Taa-dum-e-marg **ता-दम-ए-मर्ग़** Till the time of death

Taaam **तआम** Victuals/ Food

Taaat **ताअत** Act of devotion/ Obsequiousness/ Obedience/ Submission

Taab **ताब** Endurance/ Bright/Tolerance/ Warmth

Taabaan **ताबां** Bright/ Shining

Taabaanii **ताबानी** Brightness

Taabiir **ताबीर** Interpretation of dream

Taabish **ताबिश** Splendour

Taa-ba-qadam **ता-ब-क़दम** Up to step

Taahid **ताहिद** Protect

Taaib **ताइब** Repentant

Taaiid **ताईद** Encouragement

Taaiid-e-haq **ताईद-ए-हक़** Confirmation of truth

Taajvarii **ताजवारी** Kingship

Taakhiir **ताख़ीर** Delay/ Retardation/Lateness

Taakiid **ताक़ीद** Stress/ Emphasis/Pressure/ Admonition/ Injunction/Accent

Taala **ताला** Fortune

Taala-e-bedaar **ताला-ए-बेदार** Awakened fortune

Taalib **तालिब** Candidate

Taam **ताम** Food/Victuals

Taa-maqduur **ता-मक़दूर** To the best of one's ability

Taamiir **तामीर** Building/Construction/Repair/Act of construction/Erection of edifices

Taaq **ताक़** Niche/Unique

Taaqon **ताक़ों** Niches/Holes in wall

Taar **तार** Darkness/Tatters

Taaraaj **ताराज** Plunder/Devastation/Destruction/Ruin

Taasii **तासी** Cover/Make-up/Obedience/Submission/Observance

Taassur **तअस्सुर** Impression

Taassuub **तासूब** Prejudice against or for

Taauus **ताऊस** Peacock

Taaza-dam **ताज़ा-दम** Refreshed

Taaziiren **तअजीरें** Articles of law

Taaziir **तअज़ीर** Punishment

Taaziim **तअज़ीम** Respect

Tabaah-kun **तबाह-कुन** Devastating

Tabaq **तबक़** Large tray or dish/Region/World

Tabassum **तबस्सुम** Smile

Tabeeb **तबीब** Doctor

Tab-e-khud-aaraa **तब-ए-ख़ुद-आरा** Self-exhibiting nature

Tab-e-ravaan **तब-ए-रवां** Smooth nature/Mellow disposition

Tabiiii **तबीई** Natural

Tabsire **तबसिरे** Reviews

Tadaave **तदावे** Offering

Tadbeer **तदबीर** Plan

Tadriis **तदरीस** Teaching/Instruction/Education

Tafaavut **तफ़ावुत** Difference/Dissimilar/Disparity/Diversity/Distance/Geographical distance

***Tafraqa* तफ़रक़ा** Conflict/ Discord

***Tagaaful* तग़ाफ़ुल** Neglect/ Ignorance

***Tagiyaani* तग़ियानी** Flood/ Inundation

***Tahammul* तहम्मुल** Patience/Endurance/ Tolerance

***Tahayya* तहय्या** Determination/ Provision/Putting in order/Resolve

***Tahayyur* तहय्युर** Amazement/ Astonishment

***Tah-e-daruun* तह-ए-दरूं** Bottom of inside

***Tahii-dast* तही-दस्त** Impoverished hands

***Tahsiin* तहसीन** Acclamation/ Appreciation

***Tahuur* तहूर** Pure/ Purifying/Clean

***Taiin* तईं** Till (**तक** in Hindi)

***Tajaahul* तजाहुल** Ignorance

***Tajallii* तजल्ली** Splendour/ Brightness/Brilliance/ Refulgence/Lustre

***Tajdiid* तज्दीद** Renewal/ Renovation

***Takaan* तकां** Weariness/ Fatigue/Tiredness/ Motion/Movement/ Jolt/Jerk/Bump

***Takabbur* तक़ब्बुर** Pride/Arrogance/ Haughtiness/Insolence

***Takallum* तक़ल्लुम** Conversation

***Takbiir* तक़बीर** Saying God is great/Words said before the Islamic prayer begins

***Takhliiq* तख़्लीक़** Creation/ Compilation/Invention

***Takhliya* तख़्लिया** Privacy/ Solitude

***Takhmiine* तख़मीने** Estimates

***Takmiil* तक़मील** Completion/ Consummation/ Flawlessness/ Effectuation

***Talaafii* तलाफ़ी** Recompense/Redress/ Making amends/ Compensation/ Reparation

***Talab* तलब** Demand

***Talaatum* तलातुम** Storm/ Tumult/Ebb and flow/ Choppiness/Roughness of sea/Buffeting of waves

***Talkh* तल्ख़** Bitter

***Talkh-kaamii* तल्ख़-कामी** Bitterness

***Talkh-navaaii* तल्ख़-नवाई** Saying bitter things/ Unpleasant talk

***Tamaa* तमअ** Greed/ Avarice/Covetousness

***Tamaazat* तमाज़त** Intense heat

***Tamhiid* तम्हीद** Excuse/ Preamble/Preface/ Introduction

***Tamkanat* तमकनत** Dignity/Majesty

***Tanaab* तनाब** Tent-rope

***Tanaffur* तनफ़्फ़ुर** Aversion/Disgust/Utter dislike

***Tan-e-uryaan* तन-ए-उर्यां** Naked body

***Tang-daamaanii* तंग-दामानी** Narrowness

***Tanqiid* तंक़ीद** Criticism/ Fault-finding/Judgement

***Tanuur* तनूर** Oven

***Tanviir* तन्वीर** Illumination

***Tanz* तंज़** Satire/Sarcasm/ Sneer

***Tapaak* तपाक़** Cordiality/ Warmth

***Tap-e-ishq* तप-ए-इश्क़** Burning in love

***Tap-e-saudaa* तप-ए-सौदा** Heat of madness/frenzy

***Tapish* तपिश** Heat/ Warmth/Distress/ Uneasiness/Agitation

***Taqaazaa* तक़ाज़ा** Demand/Urge/Pressing settlement/ Demanding

***Taqdiim* तक़दीम** Division

***Taqliid* तक़्लीद**
Conformity/Being a conformist/To follow old ways and traditions

***Taqriib* तक़रीब** Ceremonial occasion/Function/Commemoration/Bringing near

***Taqriib-e-mulaqat* तक़रीब-ए-मुलाक़ात**
Time for meeting

***Taqreer* तक़रीर**
Speech

***Taqsiim* तक़्सीम**
Distribute/Division

***Tarab* तरब** Cheerfulness/Joy/Happiness/Mirth/Merriment/Hilarity/Violin strings

***Tarab-zaaron* तरब-ज़ारों**
Music places

***Tarah-daar* तरह-दार**
Elegant/Graceful/Beautiful/Handsome

***Tarannum* तरन्नुम** Singing/Sweet recitation/Way of singing/Words uttered in a musical tone

***Tardiid* तर्दीद** Repudiation

***Targiib* तर्ग़ीब** Temptation/Allurement/Incitement/Stimulation/Inducement/Instigation/Persuasion

***Tarjumaan* तर्जुमां**
Interpretation/Translation/Spokesperson

***Tarjumaan-e-shauq* तर्जुमां-ए-शौक़**
Interpreters of love

***Tarrar* तर्रार** Sharp/Eloquent

***Tartiib* तर्तीब** Arrangement

***Tarz* तर्ज़** Mode/Form/Style/Manner

***Tasaadum* तसादुम**
Collision/Clash/Conflict/Quarrel/Encounter

***Tasalsul* तसलसुल**
Succession/Series/Sequence/Connecting like a chain

***Tasarruf* तसर्रुफ़**
Possession/Use/Occupancy/Extravagance

***Tasavvur* तसव्वुर** Imagination/ Contemplation

***Tasavvuf* तसव्वुफ़** Spirituality/Devotion/ Abstinence from worldly pleasures/Sufism/ Spirituality

***Tasbiih* तस्बीह** Rosary

***Tasdeeq* तस्दीक़** Attesting/ Verifying/Proving true/ Athenticating

***Tashaddud* तशद्दुद** Violence/Aggression

***Tashbiib* तश्बीब** Introduction to ode/ Introductory couplet of Qasida

***Tashdiid* तश्दीद** Contravention

***Tashhiir* तश्हीर** Publicity

***Taskhiir* तश्क़ीर** Capturing/Conquering/ Subjugating/Captivating/ Subjugation of spirits

***Taskiin* तस्कीं** Consolation/comfort/ Pacifying/Soothing

***Tasliim* तस्लीम** Obeisance/ Homage/Conceding/ Acknowledging

***Taufiiq* तौफ़ीक़** God's grace/Divine guidance/ Ability/Help

***Tauqiir* तौक़ीर** Respect/ Honour/Veneration/ Reverence

***Tausan* तौसन** Horse

***Tavaaf* तवाफ़** Circling around the Kabah seven times/Going round/ Moving in circles/ Circulate

***Tavaazo* तवाज़ो** Humility/ Civility/Politeness/ Hospitality/Courteous welcome

***Tavahhum* तवह्हुम** Superstition

***Tavakkul* तवक़्क़ुल** Trust in God/Faith

***Tavajjo* तवज्जो** Attention/ Favour/Regard/ Inclination

***Tavangar* तवंगर** Rich/ Powerful

***Tavaqqo* तवक़्क़ो** Expectation

***Tavaqquf* तवक़्क़ुफ़** Delay/Hesitation/Pause

***Taviil* तवील** Long

***Tawazun* तवाज़ुन** Equilibrium

***Tazaamat* तज़ामत** Intense heat

***Taziin* तज़ीन** Embellishment

***Tazkira* तज़्किरा** Description

***Tehqeeq* तैहक़ीक़** Queries

***Tehreer* तैहरीर** Writing/Composition/Document

***Tesha* तेशा** Axe/Hatchet

***Tez-rau* तेज़-रौ** Fast-moving/Fast speed/Swift

***Thaan* थान** Stall for horse or cattle/Place to stay

***Thath* थथ** Mob

***Tibaa* तिबअ** Nature/Habit

***Tifl* तिफ़्ल** Male child

***Tiflaana* तिफ़्लाना** Childish/Childlike

***Tiflii* तिफ़्ली** Childhood/Infancy

***Tihii* तिही** Empty/Vacant/Void

***Tiinat* तीनत** Disposition/Temperament

***Tiira* तीरा** Dark

***Tiira-bakht* तीरा-बख़्त** Unfortunate/Unlucky

***Tiira-shab* तीरा-शब्** Dark night

***Tiirgii* तीरग़ी** Darkness/Gloom

***Tishna* तिश्ना** Thirsty/Longing/Pining for/Insatiable

***Tishna-kaam* तिश्ना-काम** Deprived/Thirsty/Unlucky/Hopeless/Unfortunate/Unsuccessfully

***Tishna-labi* तिश्ना-लबी** Having parched lips/Thirst/Desire/Passion

Tohfatan **तोह्फ़तन** As a gift

Tohmat **तोहमत** False accusation/Allegation

Tugyaanii **तुग़यानी** Flood/ Deluge/Inundation/ Overflowing

Tuhuur **तुहूर** Water of paradise

Tuluu-e-mehr **तुलु-ए-मैहर** Sunrise

Tunuk **तुनुक** Slender/ Weak/Thin/Slight/ Delicate

Tunuk-zarfi **तुनुक-ज़र्फ़ी** Cheapness/Irritable nature/Shallow temperament

Tund-khuu **तुण्ड-खू** Furious/Fretful/ Passionate

Turaab **तुराब** Earch/ Ground

Turbat **तुर्बत** Tomb

Turfa **तुर्फ़ा** Strange/ Agreeable/Novel/ Extraordinary/Rare/ Wonderful

Tursh **तुर्श** Sour/Acid/ Harsh/Ill-tempered

Tuubaa **तूबा** Tree with sweet fruit

Tuul **तूल** Length/Long/ Effusiveness

Tuur **तूर** Mount

U

Khvaabon ke ufuq par tiraa chehra ho hamesha
Aur main usii chehre se nae khvaab sajaauun
Athar Nafees

Had chaahiye sazaa men uquubat ke vaaste
Aakhir gunaahgaar huun kaafar nahiin huun main
Mirza Ghalib

Aanch aatii hai tire jism kii uryaanii se
Pairahan hai ki sulagtii huii shab hai koii
Nasir Kazmi

Zinda rahne ke the jitne usluub
Zindagii kat gaii tab yaad aae
Sadique Naseem

Sardii aur garmii ke uzr nahiin chalte
Mausam dekh ke saahab ishq nahiin hotaa
Moin Shadab

U

***Ufuq* उफ़ुक़** Horizon/ Region of earth

***Ujlat* उल्जत** Haste/Hurry

***Ujlat-e-kaar* उल्जत-ए-कार** Hasty

***Ujrat* उज्रत** Fee/Wages/ Remuneration

***Umaaraa* उमारा** Rich

***Umam* उमम** Peoples/ Nations/Tribes/Sects/ Followers

***Ummaton* उम्मतों** Followers

***Umr-e-raftaa* उम्र-ए-रफ्ता** Past life/Past time/ Elapsed time

***Umr-e-taabiiii* उम्र-ए-तबीई** Natural age

***Uns* उन्स** Attachment

***Unsur* उन्सुर** Element/ Part/Component/Factor

***Unvaan* उन्वान** Preface/ Introduction/Title

***Uqaabii* उक़ाबी** Hawkish/ Falcon-like

***Uqda* उक़दा** Knot/ Entanglement/Secret/ Mystery/Complicated affair/Knotty problem/ Confused state

***Uqda-kusha* उक़दा-कुशा** Problem solver/One who removes another's difficulties

***Uquubat* उक़ूबत** Punishment/ Chastisement/Persecution

***Uruuj* उरूज** Pinnacle/ Zenith/Height/ Elevation/Success/ Progress/Exaltation/ Climax

Uruus-e-bahaar **उरूस-ए-बहार** Bride of spring

Uryaani **उर्यानी** Nakedness

Ushshaaq **उश्शाक़** Lovers

Usluub **उस्लूब** Manner/Method/Way/Style

Usthukhvaan **उस्तुख़वां** Sleleton

Ustuvaar **उस्तुवार** Firm/Strong

Uyuub **उयूब** Defects/Faults

Uzr **उज़्र** Regret/Denial/Excuse/Pretext/Apology

Uzv **उज़्व** Part

V

Aankhon men terii dekh rahaa huun main apnii shakl
Ye koii vaahima ye koii khvaab to nahiin
Shahryar

Vaarafta huun aisaa men ki kuuche men butaan ke
Thahraauun jo tuk dil ko to phir paanv ukhad jaae
Mushafi Ghulam Hamdani

Taazgii hai sukhan-e-kuhna men ye baad-e-vafaat
Log aksar mire jiine kaa gumaan rakhte hain
Imam Bakhsh Nasikh

Ye vaqfa saaaton kaa chand sadiyon ke baraabar hai
Vo ab aavaaz dete hain to pahchaanii nahiin jaatii
Khalid Hasan Qadiri

'Kaif' paidaa kar samundar kii tarah
Vusaten khaamoshiyaan gahraaiyaan
Kaif Bhopali

V

Vaa **वा** To open or tell/ Expose

Vaabasta **वाबस्ता** Bound together/Related/ Connected/Dependent/ Subservient

Vaadi **वादी** Valley/Vale/ Passage/Route/Forest/ Desert/Obstinacy

Vaahima **वाहिमा** Whim/ Hallucination/Fancy/ Imagination

Vaalaa-nizhaadon **वाला-निज़्हादों** Born of superior rulers

Vaamaanda **वामांदा** Tired

Vaaraftaa **वारफ़्ता** Infatuated/Distracted/ Mad/Lost/Gone astray

Vaare **वारे** Offered

Vaashud-e-gul **वाशुद-ए-गुल** Open flower

Vaazhguunii **वाज़्हगूनी** Being inverted

Vabaal-e-dosh **वबाल-ए-दोश** Heavy burden on shoulder/Painful/Cause of trouble

Vadiiat **वदीअत** Reward

Vafaa **वफ़ा** Loyalty/ Faithfulness/ Fulfillment/Fulfilling a promise/Keeping one's promise

Vafaa-shiaar **वफ़ा-शिआर** Faithful/Loyal/Sincere

Vafaat **वफ़ात** Death/ Demise

Vafuur **वफ़ूर** Excess

Vahdat **वहदत** Unity

***Vahii* वही** Divine revelation

***Vale* वले** Yet/But/However

***Valek* वलेक** But

***Vajab* वजब** Maximum distance between thumb and little finger, around 9 inches

***Vajd* वज्द** Ecstasy/Rapture/ Excessive love/Religious or poetic frenzy

***Vajuud* वजूद** Existence/ Being/Substance/Life

***Vaqaar* वक़ार** Honour/ Reputation/Dignity/ Reputation

***Vaqf* वक़्फ़** Devoting (one's life)/Stopping/ Standing/Permanence/ Constancy/Trust/ Endowment/ Understanding/ Intelligence

***Vaqfa* वक़्फ़ा** Interval/ Interlude/Intermission/ Delay/Hiatus/Respite

***Vaqf-e-khalish* वक़्फ़-ए-ख़लिश** Engaged in pricking

***Vaqt-e-giriya* वक़्त-ए-गिरिया** Time of mourning

***Vasf* वस्फ़** Attribute/ Quality/Merit

***Vasiile* वसीले** Means/ Supports/Mediations

***Vasvase* वस्वसे** Whims

***Vaza* वज़अ** Condition/ State/Conduct/ Behaviour/Manner/ Style

***Vazaahat* वज़ाहत** Explanation/ Vivid description/ Clarification/Refinement

***Vusat* वुसअत** Expanse

***Vusaten* वुसअतें** Dimensions/Space/ Area/Latitude/ Amplitude

Y

Fazaa-e-dil pe kahiin chhaa na jaae yaas kaa rang
Kahaan ho tum ki badalne lagaa hai ghaas kaa rang
Ahmad Mushtaq

Jitne bikhre hue kaagaz hain vo yakjaa kar le
Raat chupke se kahaa aa ke havaa ne ham se
Munawwar Rana

Javaab dhuund ke saare jahaan se jab laute
Hamen to kar gayaa yaklakht laa-javaab koii
Khaleel Mamoon

Ham ishq men hain fard to tum husn men yaktaa
Ham saa bhii nahiin ek jo tum saa nahiin koii
Lala Madhav Ram Jauhar

Aur hii vo log hain jin ko hai yazdaan kii talaash
Mujh ko insaanon kii duniyaa men hai insaan kii talaash
Nazeer Siddiqui

***Yaad-dahanii* याद-दहनी** Reminder

***Yaaft* याफ़्त** Accessibility/Availability/Bribe/Earning/Income/Gain/Profit/Perquisite

***Yaara* यारा** Strength/Courage/Power

***Yaas* यास** Despair/Hopelessness

***Yagaana* यगाना** Unique/Singular/Sole/Unrivalled

***Yakbaar* यक्बार** Once

***Yakjaaii* यकजाई** Union

***Yak-jehtii* यक-जेहती** Solidarity/Unity/Unanimity/Singleness of purpose

***Yak-jehtii-e-hayaat* यक-जेहती-ए-हयात** Unity of life

***Yak-lahza* यक-लहज़ा** Once moment

***Yaklakht* यकलख़्त** All at once/Suddenly

***Yaksaan* यकसां** Same/Equal

***Yaksar* यकसर** All at once/All together/Entire/Totally/Completely

***Yaktaa* यक्ता** Matchless

***Yaqiin-e-kaamil* यक़ीन-ए-कामिल** Utmost confidence

***Yargalaam* यर्गलाम** Hostage

***Yazdaan* यज़दां** God

Z

Maanaa ki tuu zahiin bhii hai khuub-ruu bhii hai
Tujh saa na main huaa to bhalaa kyaa buraa huaa
Mohammad Alvi

Zar kaa banda ho ki mahruumii kaa maaraa huaa shakhs
Jis ko dekho vahii auqaat se niklaa huaa hai
Tauqeer Taqi

Ediyaan maar ke zakhmii bhii hue log magar
Koii chashma nahiin zarkhez zamiin se niklaa
Azlan Shah

Chale the yaar bade zoam men havaa kii tarah
Palat ke dekhaa to baithe hain naqsh-e-paa kii tarah
Ahmad Faraz

Mauquuf jurm hii pe karam kaa zuhuur thaa
Bande agar qusuur na karte qusuur thaa
Ameer Minai

Z

***Zaahid* ज़ाहिद** Hermit/Ascetic/Recluse/Devotee/Monk

***Zaanuu* ज़ानू** Part between waist and knees while sitting on the knees

***Zaar* ज़ार** Afflicted/Lamenting/Fertile land/Humble

***Zaat* ज़ात** Tribe/Caste/Breed/Origin/Essence/Sort/Kind/Substance/Nature

***Zaat-e-baht* ज़ात-ए-बह्त** The God/Holy/Pure being

***Zabh* ज़ब्ह** Slaughter/Sacrifice

***Zabuun* ज़बूं** Impure

***Zad* ज़द** Target/Blow/Range/Loss/Stroke/Object of an aim/Damage

***Zada* ज़दा** Victim

***Zadan* ज़दन** Infatuated

***Zahe* ज़हे** Excellent

***Zahid* ज़हिद** Devotee

***Zahiin* ज़हीं** Intelligent/Ingenious

***Zahmat* ज़हमत** Trouble

***Zahuur* ज़हूर** Manifestation

***Zaiifon* ज़ैफों** Weak

***Zaiff-o-zaar* ज़ैफ-ओ-ज़ार** Weak and distressed

***Zakhiira* ज़ख़ीरा** Treasure/Hoard

***Zamaam* ज़माम** Reins

***Zamaan* ज़मां** Time

***Zamaana-saaz* ज़माना-साज़** Opportunist/One who changes his principles according to the situation/Cunning

***Zamzam* ज़म-ज़म** Well in Kaba whose water is considered holy/water from this well

***Zamzama-sanj* ज़मज़मा-संज** Singer/One who sings in a melodious voice/Musician/Eulogist

***Zamzama-sanjii* ज़मज़मा-संजी** Music playing/ Sound like water falling

***Zan* ज़न** Female

***Zana* ज़ना** Bastardy/Lewd/ Infidelity

***Zanaan* ज़नान** Women

***Zanakhdaan* जनख़दां** Dimple/Pit in chin

***Zan-muriidii* ज़न-मुरीदी** Hen-pecked

***Zar* ज़र** Gold

***Zarar* ज़रर** Ruin/Damage/ Harm/Injury

***Zarb* ज़र्ब** Blow/Striking/ Multiplication

***Zard* ज़र्द** Pale/Yellow/Dull

***Zarf* ज़र्फ़** Capability/Vase

***Zar-fishaaniyaan* ज़र-फ़िशानिआं** Gold sprinkling

***Zariif* ज़रीफ़** Humorous/ Witty

***Zarkhez* ज़रखेज़** Fertile/ Rich soil/Productive

***Zau* ज़ौ** Glow/Light

***Zauq* ज़ौक़** Derive pleasure from/ Taste/Appreciation/ Enjoyment/Talent/ Verve/Relish

***Zauq-e-nazar* ज़ौक़-ए-नज़र** Perceptive eye/ Connoisseur

***Zauq-e-yaqiin* ज़ौक़-ए-यक़ीन** Gift of belief

***Zavaal* ज़वाल** Afternoon when the sun is on the decline/Decline/Decay/ Failure/Cessation

***Zeb* ज़ेब** Beauty/Elegance/ Grace/Adornment/ Adorning/Imparting grace to/Decorating

***Zeb-e-gullu* ज़ेब-ए-गुल्लू** Adornment of the neck

***Zer* ज़ेर** Under

***Zer-e-lab* ज़ेर-ए-लब** Quietly

***Zer-o-zabar* ज़ेर-ओ-ज़बर** Topsy-turvy/Upside down/To ransack/To disintegrate

***Zi-bas* ज़ि-बस** Plentifully/ In abundance

***Zihaanat* ज़िहानत** Intelligence

***Ziinat* ज़ीनत** Grace

***Ziin-saazii* ज़ीन-साज़ी** Saddling up

***Zillaten* ज़िल्लतें** Insult/Dishonour/ Disgrace

***Zindaan* ज़िंदां** Prison

***Zinhaar* ज़िन्हार** Care, Protection

***Ziyaa* ज़िया** Light/ Splendour

***Ziyaad* ज़ियाद** Increase/ Augment

***Ziyaan* ज़ियां** Loss/ Damage/Injury

***Ziyaarat* ज़ियारत** Visiting a shrine/Pilgrimage

***Ziyaarat-gaah* ज़ियारत-गाह** Place of pilgrimage

***Zoaf* ज़ोअफ़** Weak/Feeble

***Zoam* ज़ोअम** Pride/Conceit

***Zof* ज़ोफ़** Weakness/ Feebleness/Debility/ Infirmity/Imbecility of mind or body

***Zohad* ज़ोहद** Religious devotion

***Zohra* ज़ोहरा** Bright/ Beauteous/Planet Venus

***Zohra-jabiinon* ज़ोहरा-जबीनों** Venus faced

***Zor* ज़ोर** Force/Strength/ Power/Influence

***Zubuun* ज़ुबूं** Wicked/Evil

***Zuhuur* ज़ुहूर** Appearing/ Becoming visible/ Manifestation

***Zulf-e-dotaa* ज़ुल्फ़-ए-दोता** Braided hair

***Zulmat* ज़ुल्मत** Darkness/ Dark place/Region of darkness/Ignorance

Notes

Notes

Notes

Notes

Milton Keynes UK
Ingram Content Group UK Ltd.
UKHW011812260124
436745UK00004B/248